Dawn and the Surfer Ghost

Other books by
Ann M. Martin

Rachel Parker, Kindergarten Show-off
Eleven Kids, One Summer
Ma and Pa Dracula
Yours Turly, Shirley
Ten Kids, No Pets
Slam Book
Just a Summer Romance
Missing Since Monday
With You and Without You
Me and Katie (the Pest)
Stage Fright
Inside Out
Bummer Summer

BABY-SITTERS LITTLE SISTER series
THE BABY-SITTERS CLUB mysteries
THE BABY-SITTERS CLUB series
(see back of the book for a more complete listing)

Dawn and the Surfer Ghost
Ann M. Martin

AN
APPLE
PAPERBACK

SCHOLASTIC INC.
New York Toronto London Auckland Sydney

The author gratefully acknowledges
Ellen Miles
for her help in
preparing this manuscript.

Cover art by Hodges Soileau

ISBN 0-590-47050-7

12 11 10 9 8 7 6 5 4 3 2   3 4 5 6 7 8/9

Printed in the U.S.A.   28

First Scholastic printing, December 1993

CHAPTER 1

Saturday

Dear Mary Anne,,
  How are you? I'm fine—and
very busy. I miss you like
crazy! Thanks for your letter.
I got it yesterday. It's good
to hear all about what's
going on in Stoneybrook. I
miss Stoneybrook like crazy,
too, believe it or not. And
of course, I miss the BSC.
I sure wish I could be
at the sleepover at Stacey's
tonight. Oh, well. Even
though I miss everything
and everyone back in
Connecticut, I'm having a
great time here in California.
It's wonderful to be with

Dad and Jeff and my old friends. If only there were some way I could live in both places at once, life would be perfect! Anyway, I have a lot to tell you, but it'll have to wait. Right now I'm late for my surfing lesson! Can you believe it? I'm actually taking surfing lessons. More about that soon. Give my love to Richard, and give my mom a big hug for me, okay? Love always, your sister and best friend—

Dawn

Just as I signed my name to the letter, my dad called from the kitchen, "Dawn! Your ride is here!"

"Thanks!" I called back. I folded the letter I'd just dashed off, addressed an envelope, stuck on a stamp, grabbed my beach bag, and left my room. I planned to drop the letter in a mailbox on the way to the beach. I headed down the long, tiled hall that leads to the kitchen. My father was standing by the sink, drinking a glass of carrot juice he had just whipped up. " 'Bye, Dad," I said, giving him a hug.

"See you later, Sunshine," he said, hugging me back. (Sunshine is his baby name for me. Ugh.) "You be careful now, okay?"

"I will," I said. "Don't worry." Just then, I heard a car horn honk outside, and I knew that my friend's mom was getting a little impatient. "See you!" I called, as I ran out the door.

"Sorry, Mrs. Winslow," I said when I was settled in the backseat of the car.

"Oh, that's all right," she replied. "Actually, Sunny was the one who honked. She can't wait to get to the beach."

Sunny, who was sitting in the front seat, turned to face me. She grinned. "Surf's up, you know!" she exclaimed.

"Cowabunga," I said, grinning in return. Then I buckled my seat belt, leaned back, and relaxed. It was a beautiful midwinter day in California, the "Golden State," and I was on my way to the beach. What could be better?

I guess I should stop here and introduce myself. My name is Dawn Schafer, and I'm thirteen years old and in the eighth grade. I have long blonde hair and blue eyes. I guess my life might seem a little confusing to anybody else, but to me it makes sense. Let's see, how can I explain everything? Maybe I'll practice something I've been learning in English class, and make an outline. Have you ever been asked to do that? You know, with roman numerals and letters and everything? It's not easy, but it can be a good way to sort out a lot of information. So, here goes:

I. Sharon Porter, my mother, is born in Stoneybrook, Connecticut.
  A. Grows up.
  B. Has high-school sweetheart, Richard Spier, but does not marry him.
  C. Moves to California, and marries Jack Schafer.
  D. Has two children, Dawn (that's me) and Jeff (my younger brother).

II. My parents get a divorce.
  A. My mother, Jeff, and I move back to Stoneybrook.
  B. My father stays in California.
  C. I make good friends and join a special baby-sitting club (the BSC).
  D. Jeff is unhappy in Connecticut, and moves back to live with my father.

III. Mary Anne Spier (my new best friend) and I find out that her father (a widower) and my mom were those high-school sweethearts I mentioned before.

A. We set them up and they start dating again.

B. They (surprise!) fall in love.

IV. My mother remarries.
   A. My new best friend becomes my sister.
   B. We all live happily in our old Connecticut farmhouse.

V. I really, really miss my dad, Jeff, and California.
   A. I decide to go back to California for a few months.
   B. Here I am!

Phew! Pretty complicated, right? Just be glad I didn't put in all the other little things, which would have been listed under the As and Bs as 1s, 2s, and 3s. I could even have put in 1as, bs, and cs. But that would have made the outline about ten pages long. Anyway, I think you get the idea.

Being back in California has been totally cool. I love hanging out with my friend Sunny Winslow. She and I have been friends for years, so we have a special kind of bond. And after she heard about the baby-sitting club I belong to in Stoneybrook, she started one here. They welcomed me as a temporary member, which means I'm still able to do one of my favorite things: take care of little kids.

Being in California also means spending more time with my dad and with Jeff, which makes me very happy. Jeff is ten now, and I happen to think that's a really fun age. I even like Mrs. Bruen, the housekeeper Dad hired when Jeff moved back in with him. She keeps the house spotless and cooks us terrific meals. The only thing about California that I'm not crazy about is Carol Olson. She's this woman my dad has been seeing for awhile, and while I don't exactly *dislike* her, I don't love her, either. Actually, I'd probably like her just fine if she didn't happen to be my dad's girlfriend. I mean, she's young and pretty and drives a little red sportscar, and she likes MTV. She's cool, in other words. Which is fine for a regular person, but not really so fine for a woman my *father* might be serious about. Do you know what I mean? Anyway, Jeff and I have learned to get along with Carol and accept that she's in our lives for now, but that's as far as I go.

There is actually one other bad thing about California, but I've already mentioned it. It's how much I miss Stoneybrook and the people who live there, especially Mary Anne and my mom. Mary Anne is my best friend in the world, even though I haven't known her nearly as long as I've known Sunny. And my mom? My mom is a wonderful person. She may not be as organized as my dad or as neat as Mrs. Bruen (in fact, she's a completely *dis*organized slob), but she's funny and smart and very loving and — and I better not think about her any more right now or I might start feeling really sad.

And who wants to be sad when she's about to hit the beach? I was excited about going surfing that day, and nothing could ruin my mood. Sunny and I started to take surfing lessons not too long ago, when we heard that a big surfing competition was coming up. Practically all the kids at school are planning to enter at least one event, and everybody's busy preparing for it. I haven't surfed in a long time, and I was never all that good at it when I *did* do it, but I thought being involved in the competition would be a nice way to feel that I fit in with my old California friends. As it turned out, this time around I just *loved* surfing. I wouldn't have kept it up if I didn't, since "fitting in" is not as important to me as being happy with myself. Anyway, surfing is great! There's nothing like the feeling you get when you're out in the ocean, just you and your board and the waves. I can't explain it any better than that, but trust me, it's wonderful.

Sunny has been enjoying herself, too, although I think she may be enjoying the surfer *guys* more than surfing itself. She loves to hang out on the beach or in the surf shop and chat with all the incredibly cute, tanned boys. Those guys practically *live* on the beach. Surfing is everything to them, and even a pretty, smart girl like Sunny doesn't always distract them from watching for the perfect wave. This is frustrating for Sunny, I think. But she has a good time, anyway. And even though she doesn't pay as much attention as I do during our lessons, she seems to have a natural knack for the sport.

"Have fun, girls," said Mrs. Winslow. We had arrived at the beach, and Sunny and I had jumped out of the car. "I'll pick you up right here in three hours," Sunny's mom went on. "Be careful, now!"

"We will!" we chorused.

"Thanks for the ride," I added.

"Come on," said Sunny, as her mom drove off. "We have to go rent boards before all the good ones are gone."

"I'm coming," I replied. But I wasn't in a rush. First I wanted to drink in the sights and sounds of the beach. I still wasn't used to the idea that I could come here anytime (anytime I could get a ride, that is; the beach isn't exactly walking distance from my dad's house) and enjoy the warm sun, the hot sand, the blue ocean crested with white, and the seagulls that fly overhead, crying just loudly enough to be heard over the surf. I can sit on the beach and look and listen for hours. To me, it's the most beautiful place in the world. I think beaches kind of get in your blood, and if you grow up near one you never feel quite right when you're away from it.

Oh, sure, there are beaches in Connecticut. But they're not the same. The beaches on the West Coast are bigger, the surf is higher, and the sun is brighter. Plus, there's nothing like a sunset over the Pacific.

"Dawn, come *on*," said Sunny, grabbing my arm and practically *dragging* me toward the surf shop. The little building was crowded with surfers, but we fought our way through them and picked out the boards we wanted to rent. As we were standing in line to pay for them, Sunny leaned over to whisper in my ear. "Don't look now, but that's Thrash back there, working on that board."

I peeked into the back of the shop where a guy was working on a surfboard set across two sawhorses. I couldn't get a good look at him, but I could tell he was a little older than most of the high-school kids who usually hang out at the shop. "Who's Thrash?" I whispered back.

"Only the hottest surfer around," said Sunny. "He's incredible. I've seen him do some really radical stuff out there." She nodded toward the waves.

"Well, maybe if we practice hard, we'll be that good someday, too," I said. We had reached the front of the line, and we paid for our rentals. "Ready for our lesson?" I asked Sunny. We were supposed to meet Buck, our instructor, on the beach, so we grabbed our boards and ran for it.

The waves were perfect that day, and I surfed better than I ever had before. By the time I returned home I felt exhausted, but it was a good kind of tired. I had just enough energy to help Jeff with his math homework. Then, after a dinner of nachos with guacamole (I made it, since Mrs. Bruen doesn't work on Saturdays), I settled in on the living room couch and dialed my friend Stacey McGill's number. I knew from Mary Anne's letter that my friends in the BSC would be at her house for a sleepover, and I was dying to hear their voices.

Stacey answered, and I talked to her for a few minutes. Then I talked to Mary Anne and to my other friends: Kristy Thomas, Claudia Kishi, Jessi Ramsey, and Shannon Kilbourne. The only member of the BSC I didn't talk to was Mallory Pike, because she's getting over mono and she isn't allowed out for sleepovers. They told me the latest Stoneybrook news, and I told them about surfing. It was great to hear their voices. I miss them so much, and I know they miss me, too. Like I said, life would be perfect if only I could live in two places at once. But the next best thing is to feel at home in both places, and to know that the friends I have made are friends forever.

CHAPTER 2

Monday

Dear Everybody,
    I'm just about to go to a
meeting of the We ♥ Kids
Club, so of course I'm thinking
about all of you in the BSC.
You're meeting today, too, I
know. Claudia is probably
passing around Ring-Dings,
Kristy is sitting in her director's
chair, and the rest of you
are most likely chatting about
the latest adventures of
Jackie Rodowsky, the Walking
Disaster. I wish I could be
there with you. Not that I'm

craving a Ring-Ding or anything, because I still hate junk food. (Sorry, Claud!) It's just that I miss you all a whole lot. Take care!

WBS, Dawn

In case you don't know, WBS stands for Write Back Soon. I didn't really have to include that, since I get letters all the time from Mary Anne and the rest of my friends in the BSC. But those letters mean a lot to me, and I want to keep them coming. I sealed up the envelope, addressed it, and stuck a few funny stickers on the back. Then I headed over to Sunny's house for a meeting of the We ♥ Kids Club, which is the baby-sitting club Sunny started.

Sunny lives just down the street from my dad's house, so it didn't take long to walk there. When I arrived, the other members of the club were already there. Sunny had made a snack for the meeting, and everybody was digging in.

I sat down next to Maggie Blume, one of the club members. "Hi, Dawn," she said, passing me a bag of organic corn chips. "Try the spinach dip — it's great."

"It's even better with the vegetables," said Jill Henderson, holding up a piece of raw broc-

13

coli dripping with green and white dip.

Sunny passed me the platter of vegetables. "Help yourself," she said.

I took a piece of carrot and dunked it. This kind of snack is one of the reasons I like the We ♥ Kids Club. My friends and I like healthy, nutritious food — no Ring Dings for us! During BSC meetings, I always felt a little out of it when I turned down Claudia's offerings of junk food, but here I fit right in.

Don't get me wrong. It's not as if *everybody* in California is a health-food nut. Plenty of people here think that big, greasy tacos or hamburgers with fries are perfect foods. But I was brought up on mostly healthy, organic food (so were my friends here), and it just tastes better to me.

Anyway, as I mentioned, Sunny started the We ♥ Kids Club after I told her about the BSC. The California club is modeled after the Connecticut club. They're not identical, though — in fact, they're not even close. The BSC is more like a business than a club. It has officers, for one thing. Kristy Thomas, the president, is the one who came up with the idea for it. She thought it would be great if parents could reach a bunch of sitters with one phone call, and she was right. The club meets three days a week: Mondays, Wednesdays, and Fridays from five-thirty until six. That's when parents can call to line up sitters. The BSC has seven members — most of the time, that is. Lately the club has been changing a little.

Kristy is a real go-getter. She's the one who thinks up most of the ideas for the club. For example, the club record book, in which we keep track of our appointments. Also, the club notebook, in which we write up our baby-sitting experiences so the other club members can read them and stay informed about our clients. Kristy also invented Kid-Kits, which are boxes full of games, toys, and other things that kids love. They're great for rainy-day sitting jobs.

Kristy has brown hair and eyes, and she loves sports. She has a big family: her mom, two older brothers and one younger one, a stepfather, a stepbrother, a stepsister, an adopted baby sister, and a grandmother who lives with the family. Plus a dog, a cat, and two goldfish!

The vice-president of the BSC is Claudia Kishi. The club meets in her room and uses her private phone line. Claudia is Japanese-American, and she's drop-dead gorgeous, with long black hair and almond-shaped eyes. As I've told you, she loves junk food. She also loves Nancy Drew mysteries, shopping, boys, and art. Especially art. Claudia's a very talented artist, and her creativity shows in the wild way she dresses. Unlike her older sister, who is a certified genius, Claudia is not such a great student. Her parents wish she would "apply herself," but they are very understanding and supportive about her love for art.

My best friend (and sister!) Mary Anne is the secretary of the BSC. She keeps track of all our scheduling, and she does a great job. Mary Anne is shy, quiet, and sensitive. She has a boyfriend, and a kitten named Tigger. Her mom died when Mary Anne was a little girl, and her father (who is now my stepfather) was a very strict parent until recently. Fortunately, he's loosened up a lot, and now Mary Anne is treated more like a teenager and less like a little girl. Mary Anne is not only *my* best friend, but Kristy's, too. She and Kristy look a little alike, since Mary Anne also has brown eyes and hair, and is on the short side. But Mary Anne cut her hair in a cool new style recently, and now she looks trendier than Kristy.

The treasurer of the BSC is Stacey McGill. She's a whiz at math, so keeping track of our money is easy for her. She collects dues every Monday, which we use for things like paying Claudia's phone bill and buying supplies for our Kid-Kits. Stacey grew up in New York City, and she's pretty sophisticated. She has fluffy blonde hair which she perms, and she dresses *very* stylishly. Stacey's parents got divorced not too long ago, and her dad still lives in New York. Fortunately for the BSC, Stacey chose to live in Stoneybrook with her mom. Stacey is a diabetic, which means that her body doesn't process sugar correctly. She really has to watch what she eats; in fact, she is the only other member of the BSC who turns down Claudia's junk food!

Jessi Ramsey and Mallory Pike aren't officers; they're junior members of the BSC. Unlike the rest of the members, who are thirteen and in the eighth grade, Jessi and Mal are eleven and in the sixth grade. They aren't allowed to sit alone at night, so they take a lot of afternoon jobs. Jessi is African-American, and she has a little sister and a baby brother. Her great-aunt lives with the family, to help out with the kids, since both of Jessi's parents work. Jessi is a very talented ballet student, and she has the long legs of a ballerina. Mallory, who isn't attending BSC meetings these days because of her mono, comes from a huge family of eight kids! She's the oldest, so she's used to baby-sitting. Mal has curly red hair, glasses, and braces. She's in an awkward phase right now, but I think she's going to be really pretty in a few years.

The BSC also has an associate member who doesn't necessarily come to meetings, but is available if we need an extra sitter. His name is Logan Bruno, and he is Mary Anne's boyfriend. He's from Kentucky, and he has the most luscious Southern accent.

My BSC job, when I'm in Connecticut, is to be the alternate officer. That means I can fill in for anyone who's absent. The BSC has temporarily replaced me with Shannon Kilbourne, a girl from the neighborhood Kristy moved to when her mother remarried. Shannon is usually an associate member, but now that I'm away, she's more like a full-time member.

Anyway, as I said, the We ♥ Kids Club is very different from the BSC, and the snacks aren't the only example of this. The We ♥ Kids Club has no officers, no club notebook, and no regular meetings. The members just get together whenever they feel like it. Clients can call anytime, and whoever wants a job takes it. It seems to work out fine, even though it's much less organized than the BSC. The We ♥ Kids Club has one thing that the BSC *doesn't* have: a cookbook full of healthy recipes. The club members also have recipe files that they update. The kids they sit for love to spend time in the kitchen, cooking up Granola Snack Squares, Veggi Bursts, and other fun, nutritious treats.

Sunny is the only member of the club I know well. She and I have always gotten along like sisters, maybe because we've spent so much time together. Sunny's mom is like a second mother to me. Mrs. Winslow is really neat; she's a potter, and makes amazing things out of clay. She and her husband used to be hippies, I think. Sunny's real name is Sunshine Daydream, if you can believe that! (It's just a coincidence that my dad calls me Sunshine, but Sunny and I always thought that made us soul sisters.) Sunny has blonde hair, but she's not a stereotypical Californian, and none of the other members are, either. Sunny's hair is strawberry-blonde, with lots of red highlights, and she has freckles across her upturned nose. She always seems to be in a good mood, and she loves to flirt. One thing that Sunny and I have in common is that we love ghost stories. She has a whole bunch of great books, and we like to trade back and forth. And nobody can beat Sunny for telling a scary story when the lights are out during a sleepover.

Maggie Blume lives a few blocks away from Sunny and me. Her dad is involved in the movie business, but Maggie never acts stuck-up about it. Once in a while she'll mention that "Tom" or "Winona" was over for dinner the night before, but she won't make a big point of saying that it was Tom Cruise or Winona Ryder. Maggie has a little brother named

Zeke, who has been in a few commercials. The Blumes' house is huge and sprawling, and they have a pool that looks like a tropical lagoon. I guess they're rich.

Maggie has very short hair, cut in a punky style with a long tail hanging down the back. Sometimes her mom lets her dye a red or purple or pink streak in it. Her hair goes with her clothes, which are pretty wild. She likes to wear big black boots, and leather jackets over vintage dresses (from the 1950's). Maggie likes really loud rock music. But she's not punk or anything. She's a very nice girl, and a good student. She happens to love ghost stories, too, almost as much as Sunny and I do.

Jill Henderson has dark blonde hair, almost brown, and deep brown eyes that remind me of chocolate. She's quiet and self-assured, and kind of serious. Jill lives in a small house in the hills with her mother, who is divorced, and her older sister Liz. The Hendersons have three dogs that they love dearly. Their names are Spike, Shakespeare, and Smee, and they are all boxers with funny, ugly faces.

That day at our meeting, Jill was telling us how Smee likes to chase the cat next door. It makes Mrs. Banks so *mad*," she said, "so I try to keep him away from her precious Tinkerbell. But once in a while he gets away from me, and you should see how they run through the bushes. I actually think Tinkerbell enjoys being chased, but there's no way to convince Mrs. Banks of that." Jill grinned.

Just then the phone rang, and Sunny answered it. "Hold on," she said, after listening for a moment. She put her hand over the receiver. "Who wants to sit for Clover and Daffodil next Tuesday at eight?" she asked.

"I will!" I said. Clover and Daffodil are the two girls who live next door to me. They're lots of fun to sit for.

Sunny arranged the job and hung up. "Dawn, you and I had better be careful about taking too many jobs," she said. "We're going to be pretty busy with the children's program."

"I know," I said. "But Clover and Daffodil are no trouble. And I'll be back from the beach in plenty of time." Sunny and I had just gotten involved in a special children's program at the beach. It takes place on Tuesday, Wednesday, and Thursday afternoons, and most Saturdays, and it's mainly for kids with working parents. The program is a lot of fun, and it's perfect for us, because a bus takes the kids — and us — to the beach right after school. That way, we don't have to worry about rides to the beach for surfing lessons. (We have some time to ourselves after we help with the kids.) I'm enjoying getting to know the kids. Actually, I already knew three of them. One, Stephie Robertson, is an eight-year-old girl who has asthma, and the other two are brothers named Erick and Ryan DeWitt, who are real terrors. Erick is eight, and Ryan is six, and together they can truly be devilish.

"We'll have to make sure to separate Erick and Ryan tomorrow," said Sunny. "They behave much better when they're not acting as a team."

"Good idea," I said, remembering a sand-throwing fight they had started last week. I dunked another piece of broccoli into the dip and smiled. The We ♥ Kids Club might be different from the BSC, but the members of both clubs share one important quality: they understand kids and love to baby-sit. I felt right at home.

CHAPTER 3

Tuesday

Dear Stacey,
 Remember how much you liked surfing when the BSC took a vacation out here? Now I know just how you felt. I wasn't crazy about surfing before, but now I'm addicted to it. I wish you could be here with me, riding those waves!

More later—

I had been thinking of Stacey a lot lately, ever since I found out how much fun surfing could be. I remembered when my friends in the BSC came to California, after we won a lottery. That was back when I lived full-time in Stoneybrook. Everybody had a great time, and Stacey spent practically the entire vacation on the beach, learning to surf.

I had started that letter to Stacey during study hall. I should have been studying for an English quiz, but I was having a hard time concentrating. That day, after school, Sunny and I would be going to the beach to help with the children's program. And afterward, we had planned to practice our surfing. I could hardly wait.

When the last bell rang, I ran out to the courtyard to meet Sunny. I sat on a bench in the sun as I waited, and thought how different my California school is from Stoneybrook Middle School, the school my friends back in Connecticut were attending that same day.

SMS is a perfectly nice school. It's an old brick building with wide hallways and big windows in each classroom. But my school in California is totally different. It's a series of one-story buildings arranged in a star shape around a big courtyard. There are skylights in all the classrooms, so the rooms are flooded with light. The courtyard is full of plants and trees, and it looks like a tropical garden. The bench where I was waiting for Sunny is my favorite place to sit. It's near a huge bougainvillea. A bougainvillea, in case you've never seen one, is a combination of a tree and a vine, and it's covered with gorgeous pink flowers. The one in the courtyard climbs up a trellis by the window of the school library. Hummingbirds love bougainvillea, and a few were hovering around that day. Hummingbirds at school! I love California.

"Hey, girl!" said Sunny, dashing into the courtyard. "Ready to boogie?"

"You bet," I said. "We'd better run, too, if we're going to catch that bus."

To reach the beach, we had to meet the bus (really a mini-van) for the children's program at a nearby elementary school. It picks up several kids there, and then winds its way toward the beach, picking up kids at other schools on the way.

Sunny and I hurried to the school and climbed into the waiting van. Stephie, Erick, and Ryan were already in the van, with a ten-year-old boy named Tyler and a six-year-old girl named Sara. "Hi, Dawn!" called Erick, who was kneeling on his seat. "Want to see my new Turtle?" He held up a little figure.

"Nice," I said. "But I think it's time to sit

down and fasten your seat belt." The driver had climbed into the van. She closed the doors, and we were off to our next stop.

About forty-five minutes later — forty-five *long* minutes of hearing Erick and Ryan fight over the toys they had brought and listening to Stephie and a girl named Ruby (whom we had picked up at the next school) giggle endlessly — we arrived at the beach. Sunny and I slathered suntan lotion on the kids, made sure each one was holding the right beach bag, and then herded them over to the roped-off area where the children's program meets.

The program director, a woman named Alyssa, was already there, along with about twenty other kids. Alyssa's assistant, a guy named Dean, was teaching the kids how to play "Duck, Duck, Goose" in the sand, with another teen helper, Sondra. Erick, Ryan, and the other kids from our van joined in right away, and Sunny and I did whatever we could to help out with the crowd of children.

First, while the game was going on, we set out juice and crackers for a snack. Then I took one of the youngest girls to the bathroom while Sunny and Alyssa seated everyone in a circle. They passed around the juice and crackers, and tried to quiet everyone down a little. After the snack, I helped out with another game — this time it was "Twenty Questions"

— while the kids digested their food. About a half hour later, we took the kids to the bathhouse to change into their suits, and then brought them down to the water. Most of them just waded and splashed around, but a few of the older kids are good enough swimmers to venture out a little deeper. Alyssa had made sure each of the helpers knew exactly which kids they were responsible for, and we were careful to keep a close eye on them all.

Being at the beach with a bunch of kids is a lot of fun. Kids love the sand and the ocean, and they never seem to get bored or whiny. I ran and jumped with them, and tossed a beach ball back and forth. I helped them build a gigantic sand castle. I even let the kids bury me in the sand. Sunny took Stephie, Ruby, and Tyler on a beachcombing walk, looking for shells and pebbles.

After an hour or so, Alyssa told Sunny and me that we were free to go. Many of the kids had been picked up by their parents, and the rest were having quiet time under the shade of a big awning. The bus would be leaving in another hour, which left Sunny and me just enough time to rent boards and practice a little.

We headed for the surf shop. The beach was pretty crowded, and I saw a cluster of surfers near one end, where the waves were the best that day. "Looks like a good day for surfing," I said. "The waves are perfect. Not too big, but not too small, either."

Sunny grinned. "Perfect," she agreed.

We pushed open the door of the shop, and when the bell jingled the person at the counter looked up at us. It was that guy, Thrash. Sunny elbowed me, but I ignored her. I didn't want Thrash to think I was some silly kid. I wanted him to think I was cool. Like he was. Seeing him up close, I could tell that Thrash was about twenty years old, and tall — maybe six feet two — with shoulder length white-blond hair. He was incredibly tan, and his blue eyes were intense in his brown face. He had three holes pierced in his right ear and two in his left — one more than I have! (I have two in each ear.) And he wore a wild-looking copper ring that looked like a snake twining around his middle finger. I guess he was good-looking, but definitely not my type. Too wild, too old, and too — well, just too-too. Still, I found him fascinating. I wondered what his real name was. I mean, could his parents actually have named him Thrash?

Trying to look as if I knew what I was doing, I strolled over to the spot where the rental boards are kept, and started to check them over. "I've been thinking about using a bigger board," I said to Sunny. "These 'guns' are cool, aren't they?" "Guns" are what surfers call large, long boards.

"Those boards are only good for the really big screamers," said Thrash, stepping up behind me.

Screamers? I decided he must mean waves. "Oh," I said.

"You'll do best on a tri-fin, like this one." Thrash pointed to a neon pink board. "Real stable, even if you run into something gnarly out there."

Gnarly? I was going to have to study my surfer slang.

"Call me when you're ready," Thrash said. He headed back to the repair part of the shop, where I'd seen him the other day. He started to rub wax on a board (surfers use it to keep from falling off their slippery boards), and I could tell it was *his* board by the loving way he applied the wax. The board was as distinctive as its owner. It was purple, with black designs that looked like primitive tribal tattoos. I hadn't seen anything like it. I walked a little closer to Thrash so I could see what he was doing. Taking care of a surfboard is a big part of surfing, but I didn't know much about it, since I had been renting my boards.

"Cool-looking wax," I said, pointing to the can he was dipping into. The can was black, with a picture of a skull and crossbones in white on the front. I had never seen wax like that before, either.

"Custom-blended by this old guy down in Waimea," said Thrash. "I tell him what I want, and he makes it up for me. Costs a lot, but it helps me win contests, so I guess it evens out."

"Where's Waimea?" I asked.

"Hawaii," he said. "Monster waves down there. Much bigger than the ones at Kirra Point."

"Where's — ?" I began.

"Down Under. Australia," he replied, before I could ask. I realized that Thrash had probably surfed all around the world. He was one of those guys who travels everywhere in search of the perfect wave. And I had a feeling he had won a lot of competitions.

I could have hung out and listened to Thrash talk about surfing all afternoon, but I could see that Sunny was getting restless. We picked out boards, paid for them, and headed for the door.

"Take it easy, Kelea," said Thrash, grinning at me.

"Kelea?" I repeated.

"A legendary Hawaiian princess who made friends with the water god. She was a radical surfer," he said.

"Oh," I replied, blushing. "Well, thanks. I guess I better practice if I want to live up to that name."

Sunny elbowed me again as we walked to the water. "I think he likes you," she said.

"No way. He's a neat guy, though, isn't he?"

"From what I hear, he's kind of tough. The guys say he's gotten in some fights since he's been here. He doesn't care about anything except surfing, and if you get in his way, watch out." Sunny grimaced. "You better not get mixed up with him," she added.

"I won't," I said. "I just want to talk to him."

By that time, we had reached the area where the surfers were hanging out. Some kids from my school were there, and plenty from the high school, including some kids Stacey had surfed with when she was visiting. They're a little wild. Stacey even got into a car accident when she was driving to the beach with them one day. Still, they're basically good kids. "Hi, Paul," I said to one of them. "Is Alana here today?"

"She's out there," he said, pointing to the waves. "With Rosemary. Carter and I are just about to paddle out. Want to come?"

"Sure," I said. My heart was beating fast at

the very thought of riding through the waves. Suddenly, I couldn't wait to get into the water.

Stacey, you wouldn't believe the waves today, I wrote when I got home. I wanted to send off the letter the next morning, so I decided to finish it up.

Truly awesome. I wiped out once, but I held my breath and only got about three gallons of water up my nose. No problem! I'm improving, I think. Not that I'll win any prizes in the competition, but at least I won't embarrass myself. Next time I write I'll tell you about this cool surfer dude I met. His name's Thrash...

CHAPTER 4

Thursday

Dear Kristy,
   I wish you were here. Boy,
do I wish you were here.
Something terrible happened,
and somehow I think you
might be able to help me
understand it or figure it
out. You're always so practical,
and full of good ideas.
Anyway, what happened was
that this guy Thrash, a surfer,
had a terrible accident. He
might even be — oh, I can't
write the word. I just wish
I knew what to do.

It was Thursday afternoon when I heard the news. Sunny and I had arrived at the beach, all ready to have a great time with the kids in the program. Alyssa had planned some terrific activities.

Sunny and I were just getting settled at the spot where the children's program meets when Rosemary, one of the surfers from the high school, ran across the sand to us. She looked upset. "Can you believe it?" she said. "Nothing like this has ever happened on our beach. No way am I going into the water today. I mean, what if it was a shark?"

"Whoa," said Sunny. "What are you talking about?"

"You haven't heard?" asked Rosemary. "It's Thrash."

"Thrash?" I repeated, feeling scared all of a sudden. "What? What happened to him?"

"He's dead," said Rosemary.

"*What?*" cried Sunny and I together. And I added, "Dead? You're crazy. Thrash can't be dead. I just saw him yesterday."

"It happened last night," said Rosemary. "I *guess* it was last night."

"*What* happened?" asked Sunny. Both of us were just standing there with our mouths wide open. Kids from the program were running around nearby, kicking up sand that bit into my ankles, but I ignored them.

"Nobody's sure, exactly," said Rosemary. "His board washed up on the beach today, and it's all mangled. And Thrash has disappeared."

"What was that you said about sharks?" I asked.

"That's what some people think might have happened to him," said Rosemary. "The way his board was all chopped up, it looked like he could have been attacked by a shark."

I was stunned. "No way! I'm sure he's around somewhere."

"The police have been searching all day," said Rosemary. "There's no sign of him anywhere."

"But a *shark*?" asked Sunny. "There aren't any sharks here, are there?"

Rosemary shrugged. "Who knows? Anyway, maybe it wasn't a shark. Maybe he just wiped out. Maybe his board hit him on the head and he drowned in the undertow. It's pretty wicked sometimes, especially down by the break, where he likes to surf. I mean — *liked* to surf." She shrugged again. "Anyway, he won't be surfing anymore."

I couldn't believe it was true. Thrash was

the best surfer around. How could he wipe out?

"Gotta run!" said Rosemary. "Sorry for the bad news." She turned to leave.

"Wait a minute," I said. "Isn't there something we can do? I mean, to help find Thrash?"

"What can *we* do?" she replied. "The police are on the case. This is their job."

Rosemary left, and Sunny and I exchanged glances. This was upsetting news. We looked around to make sure none of the kids had heard it, and fortunately they all seemed to be involved in building a long, twisting sand dragon. Dean was supervising, while Alyssa sat under an umbrella reading to a few kids who didn't feel like playing in the sand. "Boy. I'm glad none of them heard about *that*," I said to Sunny.

Just then I felt a little hand slip into mine. There was Stephie, looking up at me. "Dawn?" she said. "What happened? Did something bad happen?"

"Oh, Stephie," I said. She was the last kid I would have wanted to hear the news. Sometimes emotional stress can bring on one of Stephie's asthma attacks. I thought fast. "Everything's okay," I said. "One of the surfers might have had a little accident, but I'm sure he'll be fine."

"Is that why everybody is over there?" Stephie pointed down the beach, to a spot where a large crowd had gathered. I saw two or three policemen, and they looked awfully strange on the beach, wearing their dark blue uniforms, surrounded by people dressed in bathing suits.

"Yup," I said. "Do you think the policemen are going to go surfing dressed like that?"

Stephie giggled. "They would look pretty funny if they did." She looked at the crowd and giggled again. "Do you think they would even wear their hats?" she said. Then she ran off to join the dragon-builders.

"Phew," I said to Sunny. "That was close. We better try not to let the kids get wind of this. Oh, and we probably shouldn't take them swimming today, just in case. But I'm almost sure there aren't any sharks. Aren't you?"

She nodded. "But it might be good to wait a day and see what the beach patrol says. I'll tell Alyssa. She's done reading that story — maybe I can get her alone for a minute."

Sunny ran off to talk to Alyssa, but I just stood and watched the crowd, which continued to grow. Several more police officers were there now. A couple of them were talking to the surfers who had gathered, and three others were walking down the beach — probably looking for clues. Then I saw two officers dragging something up off the beach, toward a police van. I squinted to get a better look. "Oh!" I said out loud, when I figured out what they were dragging. It was Thrash's surfboard. There was no mistaking it. And it sure was mangled. The fins looked broken and the nose (that's the front part) had a huge dent. Suddenly I felt a little sick to my stomach.

What if Thrash were really dead? How awful. I studied the waves crashing on the shore. They didn't *look* lethal. They were smooth and regular, and people surfed on them every day. Oh, sure, I had heard about small accidents happening once in a while, but I had never heard of anyone who had been hurt badly, let alone . . . For a minute, I thought about quitting my surfing lessons. After all, if *Thrash* could get killed riding the waves, anyone could. But then I got a grip on myself. I was just a beginner, I reminded myself, and I never tried anything fancy. I only went in the water when the surf was mild and regular, the way it was that day. And there were always lots of people around, watching out for each other. I knew I would be okay.

"Dawn!" I heard Sunny call. I jumped. I had been thinking so hard that I had almost forgotten about my responsibilities with the kids.

"Coming!" I said. I took one last look at the waves, and one more down the beach, toward the crowd. Then I joined Sunny.

"I spoke to Alyssa," she said. "She agrees with us, so we're going to keep the kids out of the water. We'll hold relay races and play Mother May I instead of swimming. Want to help me set up a course for the races?"

"Sure," I replied. Sunny and I worked for a few minutes, but I couldn't concentrate. I kept thinking about what had happened to Thrash, and I decided I had to find out more. "Sunny," I said. "I want to go down there and find out what the police are saying. Is that okay with you? If Alyssa says I can go? I'll be back in fifteen minutes."

"Sure," said Sunny, giving me a curious look. "Hey, you — you didn't have a crush on him or anything, did you?"

"Definitely not," I said. "I only talked to him once! I just thought he was an interesting person." I couldn't believe I was saying "was" instead of "is."

I walked over to Alyssa and asked if I could be excused from my duties for a few minutes. I promised to stay and work a little late that day, instead of running off to surf. She agreed, and I headed down the beach.

As I drew closer to the crowd, I could see that the police were still talking to the surfers. Surfers who weren't being questioned were standing around in groups of two and three, talking among themselves. I walked by one of those groups, hoping to hear what they were saying. Most of the good surfers were like minor celebrities on the beach, so I knew their names.

"Man, that dude was radical," said T.J., a guy with spiked brown hair and a dangling earring.

"Totally," agreed Wanda, who's one of the best surfers — male *or* female.

"He *used* to be," said this guy named Gonzo, who was wearing wildly patterned jams. "But he was over the hill. I mean, I can bust moves he never even thought of. I was going to beat him bad in that competition, and he knew it. I bet you anything he just left town so he wouldn't have to face the humiliation."

This other guy named Spanky, who wears a nose ring, nodded in agreement.

I raised my eyebrows. *That* was an interesting theory. In a way, I hoped it was true, because it would mean Thrash wasn't dead. But I hated to think he might not be the best surfer around. I figured Gonzo was probably just jealous.

I tried to listen to the police for a while, without looking too conspicuous, but I didn't pick up much information. To tell the truth, they didn't seem very worried about Thrash. I overheard one officer refer to him as "that bum," and another speculate that he had probably just moved on to the next beach.

I thought that was pretty interesting, too, and I wanted to poke around some more, but I knew my time was up, so I jogged back to the kids and joined Sunny as she supervised the relay races.

That afternoon I couldn't put Thrash out of my mind. When I returned home, I ran straight for the newspaper to see if I could find any news about the accident. There was an article on the front page! I read it eagerly, wondering what clues had been found to the mystery. And then my eye hit on one paragraph that was so interesting I read it three times. It quoted a police detective, who discussed the possibility that Thrash's board had been tampered with. He didn't say *who* might have done it, or even if he was sure it had happened, but he did say it was a possibility. From that moment on, I knew I had to find out the truth, whatever it took. I needed to learn whether Thrash's death had been an accident — or if he had been murdered.

CHAPTER 5

Saturday

Dear Dawn,
 I'm going to have to call you some night soon, that is, if my dad will let me run up the phone bill a little more. Why? Because I have a long story to tell you, about sitting for Marilyn and Carolyn Arnold. I already wrote it up for the club notebook, and it would take me a long time to write it up again.

I'll just say that there was an accident, — not a terrible one, but an accident. And it wasn't really anybody's fault — it just happened. But I think it may affect the twins' relationship. How? I'm not sure yet, but I have a feeling it will.
Talk to you soon!
Love and xxx ooo,
Mary Anne

I heard from Mary Anne the day after I received her letter. She told me the whole story. Marilyn and Carolyn Arnold are eight-year-old identical twins. The BSC sits for them pretty frequently. When we first started sitting for them, Mrs. Arnold insisted on dressing them alike and treating them almost as one person. They had the same haircut, and they shared a room which was split down the middle into identical halves. Since then, they've worked hard to establish separate personalities. Each girl always had her own interests — Marilyn plays piano, for example, and Carolyn likes science — but now they're even more distinct. Marilyn grew her hair out, and she likes to wear simple, comfortable clothes. Her room (each twin has her own room now) is yellow. And Carolyn got a cool new haircut and some trendy clothes, and *her* room is blue, with a cat motif.

Anyway, as I was saying, when I spoke to Mary Anne I heard what happened to the twins that Saturday morning. Mary Anne had a sitting job at the Arnolds', starting at ten that morning. She arrived at a quarter to (we're always punctual, since it's good for business, and we even try to be a little early when we can), and Mrs. Arnold greeted her at the door. "Oh, I'm so glad you're early," she said. "Now *I* can get going a little early, too. My meeting should be over around four, so I'll be home soon after that." She bustled around, getting ready to leave. "The girls are in the basement, and I know they can't wait to show you what they're doing down there."

Just then, Carolyn came pounding up the stairs. "Mary Anne!" she cried. "Wait till you see our gymnastics stuff!"

Mary Anne smiled. "Gymnastics stuff?"

"Me and Marilyn are taking lessons, and we love it," Carolyn explained. "So Mom and Dad got us all this neat equipment!"

Mrs. Arnold smiled at Mary Anne. "We're so happy that they have an interest in common," she said. "Just remember," she added, turning to Carolyn, "the rules about playing down there, okay?"

Carolyn made a face. "Of course," she said. "And we're not *playing*. We're working on our routines."

"Right," said Mrs. Arnold. "How could I have forgotten?" She grinned at Mary Anne over Carolyn's head. "I better run," she said, bending to kiss Carolyn. "Be good."

"I will," Carolyn answered impatiently. "Come *on*, Mary Anne." She grabbed Mary Anne's hand and dragged her toward the basement door.

Mary Anne let herself be pulled. She was curious about what kind of equipment the Arnolds had bought. Was their basement really big enough for a vaulting horse and parallel bars?

"See?" Carolyn asked, when she and Mary Anne reached the bottom of the stairs.

"Isn't this cool?" said Marilyn, running to them. "We have mats, and a balance beam, and everything!"

"I see," said Mary Anne. She looked around, impressed. The Arnolds had made the basement into a mini-gymnastics center. Besides the mats and the balance beam (which was a low one, barely six inches off the floor), a big mirror leaned against one wall, and a cassette player, obviously secondhand, sat on a table. "You're all set up here, aren't you?"

Marilyn and Carolyn grinned. Then Marilyn ran to the balance beam. "Look what I can do!" she cried, ready to step up on it.

"No, watch me!" said Carolyn, heading for the mats as if she were about to start somersaulting backward.

"Hold on," said Mary Anne. "I can't watch both of you at the same time. You'll have to take turns. Also, didn't I hear your mom mention something about rules?" She folded her arms and waited.

"Oh, right," said Marilyn.

"The rules are easy," said Carolyn. "Just like in our real gym."

"Tell me about them," said Mary Anne.

"Well, only one person is supposed to go at a time," said Marilyn, blushing a little.

"And the other person is supposed to spot the person who's tumbling or walking the beam," added Carolyn, who wore an identical blush.

Mary Anne nodded. "What does 'spotting' mean, exactly?" she asked, even though she was pretty sure she knew.

"It's, like, if Carolyn's doing a somersault, I stand near her so I can help her over if she has trouble," said Marilyn.

"Or, if Marilyn's on the balance beam, I walk beside her so she can use me for help if she needs it," said Carolyn. "Even professionals use spotters," she added. "It's the first thing we learned about."

"Well, good," said Mary Anne. "Now you just need to remember to do it, every time. Right?"

"Right," chorused the twins.

"Okay," said Mary Anne. "Let's see what you can do. Who wants to go first?"

"Me!" said both girls. Then they looked at each other and giggled. "You can go," said Marilyn. "I need a little rest, anyway."

The twins are like that, sometimes. They get along well, and they know how to share things. I think that must come from growing up with another person *right there* all the time. If you didn't learn to share, you'd go nuts because you'd be fighting every minute.

Carolyn poised herself on the mat while Marilyn stood nearby, watching carefully. Then she turned a whole series of back somersaults, and, Mary Anne told me later, she did them very well. When she was done, she stood up with a proud look on her face, pulling herself into the posture that gymnasts go into when they've finished a routine: arms up, chest out, feet together. Mary Anne clapped loudly.

"Now me," said Marilyn. She walked to the balance beam, mounted it, and began to step along it carefully with her arms out for balance. Carolyn walked next to her, and once Mary Anne saw Marilyn reach down and steady herself by touching Carolyn's shoulder. After a fairly impressive front "walkover" (she started in a back bend and then pushed up and over), Marilyn finished her "routine," jumped off the beam, and flung herself into the "finish" posture.

Mary Anne applauded. "Great job, girls," she said.

"That's not even our real routine, either," said Carolyn. "We have this whole thing we worked out, with music." She ran to the cassette player and pressed a button. An old rock song, "Tutti Frutti," came on, and Carolyn ran back to the mats to show Mary Anne the "real" routine. She mounted the balance beam, and Marilyn stood beside her.

Just then, Mary Anne heard the phone ring. "You guys be careful," she said. "I'll be right back." She ran up the stairs to answer the phone. While she was taking a message for Mr. Arnold, she noticed that the music in the basement stopped and started a couple of times. And then, as she was hanging up, she heard a sharp, short yell from downstairs. "Uh-oh!" she said. She raced back to the basement and found Carolyn lying on the floor, crying.

Marilyn was crying, too. "It's my fault," she howled. "I was supposed to be spotting her, but the tape player wasn't working right so I tried to fix it."

"I was doing a walkover, and then I fell!" wailed Carolyn. She wriggled her foot. "Oh, my ankle. It *hurts!*"

Mary Anne bent to look at the ankle. It was already swelling. "Oh, boy," she said. "Can you stand on it?" She tried to help Carolyn up, but Carolyn collapsed in a heap.

"I bet it's broken," said Marilyn, still crying.

Mary Anne thought Marilyn might be right, but she didn't say so. Instead, she and Marilyn helped Carolyn up the stairs and into a chair, propping her ankle up on another chair. Mary Anne got ice out of the freezer, wrapped it in a plastic bag, and told Carolyn to hold it on her ankle. Then she called home. "Sharon," she said to my mom. "I need help."

"I'm on my way," my mom replied, when Mary Anne finished explaining what had happened.

Next Mary Anne called Mrs. Arnold at her meeting and told her they were heading for the emergency room. By the time my mom, Mary Anne, Marilyn, and Carolyn reached the hospital, Mrs. *and* Mr. Arnold were there, too.

Carolyn's ankle wasn't broken, fortunately. But it was badly sprained, and she was sent home with crutches and told to stay off it for awhile. As they were all leaving the hospital, Mary Anne heard Marilyn say something that took her by surprise. She told me on the phone that night that she thought the twins' relationship was going to be closer than ever from now on. Maybe *too* close.

"I'm *sorry*," Marilyn had said, sniffing. She was talking to Carolyn. "It's all my fault, and I swear I will never, ever, *ever* leave your side again."

CHAPTER 6

Dear Claudia,
  I wish you were here to
help me figure out what
to wear to this party I'm
going to tonight. It's a
beach party, so it's not
exactly formal, but I do
want to look nice. And I
have to think about layers,
since it gets cool on the
beach as the sun goes
down. I know you'd come
up with something fantastic,
but I guess since you're not
here to help me I'll just
wear my usual outfit:

shorts and a T-shirt, with
sweatpants and a big white
sweater for later. Maybe
I'll add those cool seashell
earrings you made for me!
Love, Dawn

Sunny and I were excited about the beach
party. It was sponsored by the beach club, the
one that runs the children's program. All the
kids would be having a cookout on the beach
while their parents attended a luau in the club
dining room. (A luau, in case you don't know,
is like a barbecue, Hawaiian style.) Alyssa,
Dean, Sondra, Sunny, and I had put a lot of
planning into the kids' cookout, since we
wanted to make it extra special for them.
Sunny had called me at least three times that
Saturday, to make sure we had everything we
needed. We were bringing hot dogs and hamburgers, tofu dogs and veggie burgers. We
were going to make s'mores over the campfire.
And we were brushing up on our favorite
ghost stories, so we could tell them after dark-
ness fell.

That evening, Sunny and her mom picked
me up at Dad's house. I had, with Alyssa's
permission, invited Jeff to our cookout, but he
had decided not to come. He was planning to

hang out with his skateboarding buddies, instead.

"See you guys!" I called to my dad and Jeff, as I gathered my stuff together and ran to the car. I jumped into the backseat, and Sunny turned to grin at me.

"It's a perfect night for a beach party," she said. "This is going to be great."

"You girls aren't going to go into the water, are you?" asked Sunny's mom, looking a little worried.

"No way," I said. "It's too cold at night for swimming."

"I plan to stay near that campfire," said Sunny.

By the time we arrived at the beach, most of the kids were already there, gathered around the fire pit that Alyssa and Dean had dug. The older kids had been put to work gathering driftwood, and the younger ones were playing tag around the growing pile that would soon be a bonfire.

"Dawn! Sunny!" said Alyssa. "Just in time. Sondra was about to take some of the kids on a beach clean-up walk, and Dean is going to show another group how to make seashell chimes. Why don't each of you join a group, and help out?"

Sunny set off with Sondra, Ruby, Stephie, and about six other kids. They were armed with rakes and shovels and bags for collecting garbage. "It's important to keep the beach clean," I heard Sondra saying as they walked off. "It's everybody's responsibility. See this?" She picked up a set of plastic rings that had once held together a six-pack of soda. "A fish or a turtle can get tangled up in this and die." She put it into her bag, and led the kids down the beach. I watched them go, and saw them stooping every few steps to pick things up and put them into their bags.

Dean and I led the other group of kids, which included Sara, Erick, and Ryan, in the opposite direction, to search for shells. Since we were going to make wind chimes, Dean told us to look for shells with holes in them. He was carrying a large bucket for collecting, and as the kids dropped shells in it he told us what kind they were and what type of animal had lived in them. Dean seemed to know a lot about marine life. When I asked him why, he told me he planned to be a marine biologist someday. "I want to make sure all these species survive," he said, holding a delicate shell in his hand so I could see the colors in it.

Erick and Ryan were behaving pretty well, for once. "See what I found?" asked Erick, running to me with a shell.

"Beautiful," I said. It *was* beautiful. It was

white, with a creamy pink interior.

"It's for you," said Erick shyly. Then he ran off.

"I think somebody has a crush," Dean said, with a grin.

I blushed and bent my head to look for more shells. Soon, we had gathered a big bucketful, and we turned back. Near the bonfire site, Dean had set up a work area. There were pieces of driftwood to hang the shells from, and fishing line to tie them with. We started the kids on their chimes, and soon we were busy helping to thread line through holes in the shells, tying knots, and advising kids on how to arrange the shells so that the wind would bump them together.

After awhile, Sunny and Sondra returned with their group. The kids were proud of all the garbage they had gathered. Each one was lugging a full bag, and Sunny and Sondra were carrying extras. "*That* part of the beach is a lot cleaner," said Sunny with satisfaction.

"But we would have to do that every single day, over the whole beach, to really keep it clean," said Stephie, a little dejectedly. "Now I understand why it's bad to leave even just one little paper cup on the beach. What a mess!"

Sunny and Sondra and I started talking about making posters that would let other beachgoers know why it was important not to litter. The kids thought that would be a great project, and before long we had planned a program of beach activities for the following week.

Alyssa joined us after awhile. "It's getting near dinnertime," she said. "Sunny and Dawn, would you two lay out those blankets so we can sit on them while we eat? Dean and Sondra and I will start the fire and get the food ready for the barbecue."

"Sure," I replied. Sunny and I set to work. Enticing smells were already drifting out of the beach club dining room, where the luau was under way. I was hungry, and the thought of a veggie burger hot off the fire kept me working fast. By the time Sunny and I had finished our job, the fire was ready to be lit.

"Stand back, everybody," said Dean. He bent to light the fire, and the dry wood caught immediately.

"Ohh!" said the kids, as they watched the flames rising into the darkening sky.

"Pretty!" said Stephie. "And warm." She held her hands out toward the fire. The sun was going down, and I noticed that there was a chill in the air. A thin white mist was beginning to rise over the ocean. Sunny and I got busy matching kids up with their sweaters and jackets and helping the younger ones button and zip.

Erick and Ryan and some of the other kids began a wild dance around the bonfire, yelling and throwing their hands in the air. Alyssa shook her head, smiling. "Might as well let them go to it," she said. "They'll burn off some energy." The younger kids chose a blanket near the fire and sat quietly, watching the flames.

It wasn't long before the fire had burnt down enough to cook on. Sunny and I skewered hot dogs on sticks and held them over the coals, while Dean set up a grill for burgers. As each round was finished, we passed the food out to the kids, who wolfed it down as fast as we could cook it. Finally, they had all been fed. Then we ate our own dinner, and I have to say that I've never had a veggie burger that tasted quite so good. The combination of a busy evening, the salt air coming off the ocean, and the warm, glowing bonfire seemed to make me incredibly hungry.

The kids settled into a quieter mood as we began toasting marshmallows for our s'mores. Some of the younger ones even dozed off. I saw Ruby sleeping with her head on Stephie's lap. Sunny and I walked around the circle of kids, making sure everyone was warm and cozy. I put on my sweatpants and pulled a big sweater over my head. The moon was rising by then, and the beach had become eerie looking and chilly.

"Time for ghost stories," said Alyssa, her face alight in the glow of the fire. "Anybody know a good one?"

"I do! I do!" said Erick. "Can I go first?"

Alyssa nodded, and Erick began that old tale about the spook who's walking up the stairs, step by step, slowly, slowly — until he *gets you*! The kids shrieked and giggled at the surprise ending. Then another boy named Justin began to tell a story about a swamp monster that glowed in the dark.

I smiled over at Sunny. I was pretty sure she was thinking what I was thinking — this was the perfect setting for ghost stories. Of course, the stories that the kids were telling were fairly tame, not like some I know. I think I've read every ghost story in the world, and I prefer the really scary ones. But no ghost story is as good as a real ghost. I thought about the ghost that might haunt my old farmhouse back in Stoneybrook. There's a secret passage in that house — did I mention it? — and some people think the ghost of the crazy son of one of the previous owners may haunt it. His name is Jared Mulray, and he's supposed to have died of a broken heart. I'm pretty sure I've heard him once or twice, but I haven't had an actual sighting yet. If I do, it will be one of the best moments of my life — even if it scares the pants off me.

My thoughts were interrupted by a cry from Erick. "Look at that!" he said, pointing out toward the ocean. I turned to look, and caught a glimpse of a faraway movement, though it was hard to make out much through the mist.

Within seconds, everybody was on their feet. (Everybody except the little kids who were asleep, of course.) We stared out at the breakers, trying to figure out what we were seeing.

"It's a surfer," Sunny said under her breath.

"But why would anybody be surfing on this kind of night?" wondered Alyssa.

Alyssa was right. It was hardly an ideal night for surfing, with all that mist. And even with the moon shining, it was pretty dark.

I looked again, but I couldn't see anything this time. Erick began to run, leading a group of kids along the beach toward the last place we had seen the figure. Sunny and I followed them. By the time we arrived at the edge of the water, nothing was to be seen out on the ocean.

"A ghost!" said Erick. "It was a ghost, I bet you anything."

"A surfer ghost?" said Sunny.

"I bet it's the ghost of Thrash," I said quietly. I was hugging myself, trying to stay warm. Suddenly, I couldn't stop shivering.

We herded the kids back to the bonfire, trying to calm them down so that they wouldn't scare any younger kids who had woken up.

Soon after that, the beach party ended. Alyssa gave Sunny and me a ride home, and on the way we discussed the "surfer ghost." Even though Sunny loves ghost stories, she doesn't believe in *real* ghosts. She and Alyssa were positive there was a perfectly good explanation for whatever we'd seen. For example, Alyssa thought it might have been a dolphin.

But I wasn't so sure.

Over the next week, the kids at the beach program were full of speculation about the surfer ghost. The story grew, and soon other people were reporting sightings. Even at school, it was all anybody talked about. I think a lot of people were just having fun with the story, but I took it seriously. I *knew* I had seen something that night. It *looked* like a ghost. And if it was a ghost that surfed, it could have been the ghost of Thrash. His spirit might be haunting our beach. This could be the best ghost story yet!

CHAPTER 7

'Friday

Dear Jessi,
    Boy, have I got a mystery
on my hands! And maybe
a really good ghost story, too.
I wish you and everyone
in the BSC could be here
to help me figure this one
out. How's good old Stoneybrook? I miss it—and
you, too.
                    Love, Dawn

I was trying to write regularly to all my friends back home, even though telling them everything that was going on was becoming harder. Too much was happening to be able to write it in one letter. What I really needed was to sit down with my friends and go over the facts, which is what I would do if I were back in Stoneybrook. The BSC has a great record for solving mysteries. But this time, I was on my own. Oh, I had Sunny and the We ♥ Kids Club, but it just wasn't the same. First of all, Sunny flat out refuses to believe in ghosts. And she and Maggie and Jill don't seem to get as excited about mysteries as my Connecticut friends do.

No, if I were going to find out what had happened to Thrash, I would have to do it by myself. I had thought about it a lot since the day I heard he had vanished. The sighting of the ghost surfer, and the talk about it afterward, only added to my curiosity. Here's what I was thinking: First of all, Thrash had disappeared without a trace. Second, I had seen his mangled surfboard. Third, I had read in the paper that the police believed the board might have been tampered with. And fourth, a ghostly surfer was now riding the very waves that Thrash had last ridden.

Conclusion? Don't think I'm silly, but I had begun to believe that Thrash had been murdered and his spirit was going to haunt the beach until the murderer was caught. That's a pretty common theme in ghost stories. Somebody gets stabbed, or poisoned, or whatever. The murderer thinks he has committed the perfect crime, and will never be found out. He goes on his merry way. But *then*, things begin to happen. He starts seeing images behind him in the mirror, or a hand appearing out of nowhere. Or he hears footsteps, and eerie wails. Books start to fall out of his bookshelves, all by themselves, and doors open even when nobody is around. Eventually, of course, the murderer is driven completely crazy by all this stuff, and he runs to the nearest police station and confesses everything. He's arrested, and the ghost of the murdered person is finally at rest.

I figured that whoever murdered Thrash might be feeling tortured by the fact that a surfer ghost was riding the waves at the beach. But obviously, he (or *she*) wasn't feeling tortured *enough*, because he hadn't confessed yet. That left it to me to discover who the guilty party was, and to help matters along. After all, being a spirit wandering around waiting to be put to rest can't be too much fun. Thrash might have been a surfer bum, but he deserved a better fate than that.

For more than a week after the beach party, I thought about the mystery every day. I thought about it as I was brushing my teeth in the morning, and as I sat in homeroom at school. I thought about it through my classes — and almost failed a math quiz! I thought about it while I was working at the beach program, but I made sure to watch closely over the kids I was responsible for at the same time. And at night, I dreamed about it. I dreamed about a surfer ghost, knifing through ghostly waves on a ghostly surfboard. One morning I woke up giggling because I had been wondering, in my dream, whether the ghost wore glow-in-the-dark jams when he surfed.

But all that thinking wasn't getting me anywhere. It was time to take action. I decided that I should talk to the police and make sure I wasn't missing any important information.

One afternoon, toward the end of our shift at the beach program, I told Sunny I was going to skip our surfing lesson that day.

"Why?" she asked. "You're getting really good, and Buck says it's important to keep practicing now, with the competition coming up soon."

"I know," I replied, "but I have to do something really important. I want to talk to the police about Thrash."

"Oh, Thrash," said Sunny, giving me an exasperated glance. She had decided I'd been madly in love with Thrash, and that I wasn't "over" his death. "You have to let him go," she said. "Get on with your life."

I had given up on trying to tell Sunny that Thrash hadn't been my type. I had also given up on trying to convince her to help me solve the mystery. She just didn't seem all that interested. "I really need to do this," I said firmly. "It's important to me."

Sunny shrugged. "Okay. Should I tell Buck you'll be there tomorrow?"

"Sure," I said, even though I wasn't positive I would be. That would depend on what I found from the police.

When I was finished at the beach program, I walked to the police station, which is a few streets away from the beach. The station looked a lot different than the one in Stoneybrook. For one thing, among the regular patrol cars parked outside were several dune buggies painted in police colors. Around here, the police have to patrol the beach as well as the streets. And when I went inside, I noticed that the atmosphere was a little more informal than in Connecticut. The officers wore short-sleeved uniforms. They seemed pretty friendly, too.

"What can I do for you?" asked the officer at the front desk.

"I'm interested in the case of the surfer who disappeared," I said. I had already decided that I wouldn't say anything to the police about a surfing ghost. I didn't want them to think I was a nut.

"Surfer, surfer," muttered the officer. "Can you be more specific?"

"You know," I said. "That guy whose board washed up on the beach. Thrash."

"Oh," said the officer, leaning back in his chair and folding his hands behind his head. "You mean that drifter." He grinned. "What about him?"

I frowned. The officer didn't seem to take the case very seriously. "I just wanted to know if there were any new leads."

"Leads?" he repeated. He shook his head. "Usually these things just blow over. I don't think anybody's even filed a missing-person's report on the guy."

"But — but — he's gone!" I said. "And his surfboard might have been tampered with. I wanted to find out what might have happened, like if there were high tides that night, or if there's some way to trace the damage that was done to his board."

By this time, another policeman had joined the first. He listened for awhile, shaking his head. The one at the desk was barely paying attention. He was filling out some kind of paperwork now, checking a file on his desk for information. I glanced down at the notebook I was carrying. I didn't think I would be getting any information to write in it. And then I heard the second policeman mutter something to the first.

"If he washes up, he washes up," was what I thought I heard him say. I looked at him, surprised, just in time to catch the two men grinning at each other.

Obviously, the police didn't care what had happened to Thrash. I was mad, but I knew there was no point in yelling at them. Instead, I just said, "Thank you," as frostily as I could, and left.

I didn't take any surfing lessons for the rest of that week. I spent all my free time at the beach investigating the case on my own. I talked to the surf-fishermen and learned about the tides. I talked to Gonzo and the other surfers about how the waves broke on the shore. And I talked to the beach "regulars," the brown-skinned older men and women who spend all day, every day, on the beach.

Soon, I had figured out that *if* Thrash's body had washed up on the beach, it would have been down near the old pier, where big wooden pilings were still sticking out of the shallow water. I searched the area, hoping to find some sign of Thrash. I knew I would have heard if his body *had* washed up, and I certainly wasn't expecting that it would now. But maybe I would find *something*.

One day, when she didn't have a lesson, Sunny came with me on my tour of the beach. I told her what I was looking for.

"I don't know what you're trying to prove," she said.

"I'm not sure myself," I answered honestly. "I guess I'm trying to prove that Thrash really is dead, and that he was murdered. And I'd like to figure out who did it."

Sunny shook her head. "Just like Nancy Drew!" she said. "Aren't you afraid of getting mixed up with murderers?"

"I'll go to the police when the time is right," I said. "If and when I have any evidence. Meanwhile, nobody's going to worry about some teenage girl who looks like she's beachcombing."

"That's true," said Sunny.

We walked along quietly for awhile, without finding anything. We had made our way down to the old pier, and now we were working our way back to the spot where the surfers usually head into the water.

"Hey, look at this!" Sunny cried suddenly. She bent down to pick up something. "I almost stubbed my toe on it. Why do people dump all their junk on the beach? I don't think those posters we made have helped at all."

I took the object from her hand and examined it. I had known what it was from my first glance at it, but I wanted to be sure. "Do you know what this is?" I asked, holding up the small black-and-white can. "It's Thrash's wax. His personal, custom-made wax. Nobody else uses this."

Sunny looked at me wide-eyed. "What are you trying to say?" she asked.

"I don't know," I said. "Maybe the ghost is using it."

"Oooh!" said Sunny. "Scary! But unlikely. Maybe Thrash isn't really dead, and *he's* using it."

"Not dead?" I said.

"Yeah, maybe he faked his own death, like Gonzo said. Or maybe he got hurt, and he has amnesia from bumping his head."

"Right." I grinned. "I think you may be watching too much TV. Anyway, this doesn't prove anything. It's a little dented and rusty. It could have been lying there in the sand since before Thrash disappeared."

"That's probably it," said Sunny. "So, are we done being detectives for the day? I'm hot, and I could use a swim."

We tore off our T-shirts and ran into the cool

water. I tried to let the waves wash my brain clear of all the confusing clues — or *non*-clues — I had found, but I knew that I couldn't forget about the mystery. I had to keep investigating. I had to find out what had happened to Thrash.

CHAPTER 8

Tuesday

Dear Dawn,

How are you? We miss you so much. I hope your lessons are going well. I just got back from a sitting job at the Arnolds' and I'm about to write it up for the club notebook, but I have a feeling you'd get a kick out of hearing what's going on with them. I *guess you know what happened when Mary Anne sat for them awhile back. Well, you'll never believe what's happening now ...*

Jessi wrote me a long, funny letter about her experiences at the Arnold house that day. She knew, of course, about Carolyn's accident and what Marilyn had said about "never leaving" her twin's side. She had read the entry in the club notebook. But she was still unprepared for what she saw that afternoon.

She arrived on time at the Arnolds' and rang the bell. From inside, she heard Mrs. Arnold call, "Marilyn, would you let Jessi in? I'm busy getting ready to go."

Jessi waited for what seemed like a long time. She was beginning to wonder if Marilyn had heard her mother. Maybe she was in the basement, practicing her gymnastics routine. But then, she heard noises in the front hallway — an uneven thumping sound, and a voice saying, "That's right, just take it easy. Good! Good!" And then Marilyn opened the door.

"Hi, Jessi," she said. Carolyn was standing beside her, leaning on her crutches and panting a little. "Hi," she said, when she had caught her breath.

"Hi, you guys," Jessi replied. "Thanks for letting me in. But you *both* didn't have to come to the door."

"Yes, we do," said Marilyn. "Wherever I go, she goes. And wherever she goes, I go. We stick together. Anyway, the doctor said it was good for her to exercise a little and not just sit around all the time."

Carolyn nodded. She looked tired, but she was smiling.

"How's your ankle?" asked Jessi. She's had a few sprains and other injuries herself, mostly from landing wrong in ballet class. And she knows how annoying they can be.

"It's much better," Marilyn answered for her sister. "The doctor says it's healing just fine."

Jessi grinned. "Thanks for the report, Nurse Marilyn. But I asked Carolyn. So, *Carolyn*, how is it?"

"Not too bad," said Carolyn. "At first it was keeping me awake at night, but it doesn't hurt so much anymore."

"That's good," said Jessi. "You'll be off those crutches in no time."

"She's getting really good at them," said Marilyn. "And I can use them, too. Want to see?" Carolyn handed her a crutch, and the two of them hopped up and down the hall on one crutch each, giggling and shrieking as they went.

"Girls, girls," said Mrs. Arnold, running down the stairs. "How about some quiet time now? I think Carolyn could use a rest."

"That's right," said Marilyn, in her "nurse" voice. "You need a rest, now. Come on into the living room, and I'll get you settled." She gave the crutch back to Carolyn and led her along the hall, walking very slowly so that Carolyn could keep up.

"Well," said Jessi to Mrs. Arnold, "Marilyn seems to be taking good care of her sister."

Mrs. Arnold rolled her eyes. "You don't know the half of it," she said. "But you'll see how things are. I have to run. Would you make sure the girls get their homework done? Also, Marilyn needs to practice the piano, and Carolyn has a science project to work on. They can have a snack first, though."

With that, Mrs. Arnold was gone, and Jessi was left alone with the girls. She headed into the living room to check on them, and found Carolyn lying on the couch propped up by five big pillows. Marilyn was fluffing up the sixth, getting ready to arrange it under Carolyn's head.

"Wow, you look pretty comfortable," said Jessi.

"She is," said Marilyn.

"I am," agreed Carolyn, smiling. She seemed to appreciate the attention her twin was giving her.

"Are you guys ready for a snack?" asked Jessi.

"Sure!" said Marilyn. "I'll help you get it. Or — no, I better stay here with Carolyn."

"It's okay," said Carolyn.

Marilyn looked torn, so Jessi spoke up. "Why don't I fix your snacks," she said. "I'll let you know when they're ready." She went into the kitchen and put some graham crackers on a plate. Then she poured two glasses of milk and laid out two bananas. "All set!" she called to the girls.

Marilyn came running. "I'll bring Carolyn's to her," she said. She kept looking over her shoulder, back toward the living room, as if she were worried that Carolyn might disappear while she was away. In a flash she set the cookies and milk and fruit on a tray. She added a vase with a red silk rose and stood back to see how it looked. "Perfect!" she said, picking it up.

Jessi raised her eyebrows. Then she followed Marilyn back to the living room and watched as Carolyn accepted the tray. Carolyn seemed to be getting used to her princess treatment.

"Would you like me to turn on the TV?" asked Marilyn. "You can choose whatever channel you want," she added generously.

"Let's not turn on the TV," said Jessi. "You guys have homework and piano practice and stuff."

"Okay," agreed the twins. They ate their snacks, talking excitedly about a birthday party they were going to that weekend. When they were finished, Jessi said, "Why don't I help Carolyn with her homework upstairs, and Marilyn, you can start on your practicing."

"*I'll* help her," insisted Marilyn. "I'm the only one who knows how."

Jessi didn't want to start an argument, so she let Marilyn help Carolyn up the stairs and into Carolyn's bedroom. Jessi smiled as she looked around the room. She had forgotten, she wrote me later, about Carolyn's decorating scheme — a shaggy blue rug, and blue-and-white-striped wallpaper. The matching curtains and the bedspread were printed with little black and white cats, and on the bed were two pillows in the shape of cats. Jessi even saw a cat wastebasket with pointy cat ears and a furry tail. But one thing in the room did not belong there. It was a cot, next to Carolyn's bed.

"What's the cot for?" Jessi asked.

"That's where *I've* been sleeping," said Marilyn. "My room is too far away from Carolyn's. I want to be sure I'm here if she needs me in the night."

Jessi nodded. She was beginning to understand. Marilyn had been one-hundred percent serious when she said she would never leave her sister's side. What was amazing to Jessi was how well Carolyn seemed to be taking her twin's protectiveness. Jessi wrote to me that she, herself, would have gone crazy if someone had been hovering over her all the time. But Carolyn seemed perfectly content to be waited on every minute and to have her twin nearby all day.

"So, tell me about your science project," Jessi said to Carolyn. Marilyn walked to Carolyn's desk, picked up a small light bulb, and started to explain to Jessi how her sister was making a tiny generator set.

"Aren't you supposed to do science projects on your own?" Jessi asked Carolyn. "I mean, without help?"

Carolyn nodded. "She's not really helping

me," she said. "I know much more about science than she does, anyway. But when I need a part or something she gets it for me."

"Well, how about if we leave you to work for awhile?" Jessi said. "Marilyn needs to practice for her piano lesson."

"No way!" said Marilyn. "I'll do that later, when Carolyn can be downstairs, too. I can wait while she does her stuff."

Jessi rolled her eyes. "Marilyn, don't you have homework, too?" she asked. "How about if you bring it in here?" Her suggestion seemed to please Marilyn, and before long the twins were elbow-to-elbow at Carolyn's desk, working quietly together. The girls didn't have much space, but they looked happy.

After about an hour, Carolyn said that she needed an extra part for her generator and that she couldn't do anything else until she had it. "I'm done with *my* work, too," said Marilyn.

"Great," said Jessi. She had been sitting quietly in a corner of Carolyn's room, reading a Mrs. Piggle-Wiggle book she had taken from the shelf. "I guess we could go downstairs, then, and Marilyn can practice."

They headed down the steps (with Marilyn sticking close to Carolyn in case she needed help), and Marilyn hurried to set up a chair and pillows for Carolyn next to the piano bench. Carolyn made herself comfortable in the chair, and Marilyn fetched her a book to read. Then, finally, she settled in to practice.

Marilyn is very good at the piano — she's been taking lessons since she was four — and according to Jessi, the next half hour was very pleasant. She and Carolyn sat and read while Marilyn played through the pieces she was working on for her lesson.

Afterward, they decided to play a game of Go Fish. As she picked up her cards, Jessi found herself wondering how Marilyn managed to take care of Carolyn all day at school. There was no way she could be near her every second during a school day. Finally, Jessi's curiosity got the better of her, and she asked, "Marilyn, how do you take care of Carolyn at school?"

Marilyn giggled. "I try to stay near her as much as I can," she said. "But when I can't be with her, Gozzie takes care of her."

"Gozzie?" repeated Jessi.

"Gozzie Kunka," said Marilyn. "She's a good friend of mine."

That was when Jessi remembered that Gozzie Kunka was an imaginary friend that Marilyn had made up once when the twins weren't getting along very well. She smiled at Marilyn. "That's great," she said. "I bet Gozzie does a good job."

Carolyn nodded, smiling. "She's fun," she said. "But I like Marilyn better."

Jessi could see that, Gozzie Kunka or no Gozzie Kunka, Marilyn was going to stick pretty close to Carolyn for quite a while.

CHAPTER 9

Saturday

Dear Mallory,

How are you feeling? You must be tired of being sick. It's too bad mono has to last so long. Do you miss baby-sitting? Are your brothers and sisters taking good care of you and bringing you bon-bons to eat while you lie around reading all day? I wish you could visit me here and lie in the sun — it would probably make you feel a lot better. Then again, things are pretty exciting here lately, and *the action might be too much for you. You won't believe what happened at the beach today....*

I wrote that letter to Mallory when I returned home from the beach on Saturday evening. It had been a beautiful day, sunny and warm. I had spent the morning working at the beach program, with Sunny. The kids had just about worn us out, and when the program ended we practically collapsed, glad we had decided to spend the rest of the afternoon just relaxing. We set up a spot in the sand with our blankets laid out neatly and our thermoses of juice close by. Then we sat back and watched the waves for awhile.

"Hey, guys!" said Jill, from behind us. She and Maggie were floundering through the sand, weighted down with blankets and beach bags. Jill's sister Liz had driven them to the beach to meet us, and the plan was for Liz to pick us up at the end of the day and drive us home.

"We brought some great munchies," said Maggie, setting her bag down next to me.

"We could stay here for a week, with all this food," said Jill, laughing. "Maggie fixed sandwiches, and I made oatmeal cookies. Plus, we brought a whole bunch of fruit."

I realized I was starving, and I guess Sunny was, too. We helped ourselves to sandwiches and offered our juice to Maggie and Jill. For awhile, nobody said a word. We were too busy eating.

"How come you guys aren't surfing today?" asked Jill, when she had finished the last bite of her sandwich.

"We decided to take a day off," Sunny answered. "The waves seem a little high." We looked out at the waves. They *were* high, but plenty of surfers were out. The really good surfers love to ride those screamers. As I mentioned before, they use extra-large boards, called guns, when the waves are big. Actually, some surfers call those boards rhino-chasers. Great name, isn't it? I think surfing slang is almost as much fun as surfing itself.

"The contest is still on, isn't it?" asked Maggie. "I heard a rumor that it was going to be cancelled." Maggie and Jill like horseback riding better than surfing, but they pay attention to a good surfing rumor when they hear one.

"No way!" said Sunny. "It's definitely on."

"But some people are dropping out," I added. "They think the contest is jinxed or something. Because of Thrash disappearing."

"Not just that," said Sunny. "What about all the accidents?"

There had been several minor accidents in the past week or so. A couple of surfers had been hurt, but neither of them badly. Some people said it was just coincidence. Others claimed that the ghost of Thrash was responsible, that he was haunting the beach and trying to mess up the contest. Guess which theory *I* believed? Right. I was still convinced that Thrash would haunt the beach until his murderer was exposed and justice was done. But I didn't know how to find out who the murderer was.

"Check out Paul!" cried Sunny suddenly, pointing toward the waves. "He's really carving that breaker!"

Carving, in case you're wondering, means surfing very well. And a breaker is a wave, of course. I watched Paul surf toward shore. He did look good. He and Carter had been practicing nonstop for the competition, and I had a feeling he might do well.

I leaned back and studied the surfers for awhile, enjoying the sight. The more you know about surfing, the more fun it is to watch. After all the lessons I had taken and all the practicing I had done, I could appreciate how hard just standing up on a surfboard is, much less looking cool doing it. And I was really impressed by the moves some of the guys could do. It was as if they understood the waves, and could use each one to do exactly what they wanted. They had perfect balance, and could make the boards turn through the waves so they looked as if they were cutting through butter. And at the ends of their rides, most of them executed this great move called a kick-out, a quick, short turn in which you step to the back of the surfboard and get off the wave. It looks incredibly cool.

Of course, *I'm* more likely to take a nosedive with my board at the end of a ride, and fall headfirst into the water! I'm sure everybody who sees me surf knows I'm a grommet. That's what experienced surfers call *in*experienced surfers. I try not to let it bother me. After all, everybody has to start somewhere. Every surfer was a grommet once, I figure.

I picked up a handful of sand and let it trickle through my fingers. I thought about Thrash, and how even he had once been a grommet. After a lot of practice and hard work, he had become one of the best surfers around. And now he was gone. It didn't seem right. I turned away from the waves and picked up a book of ghost stories Sunny had lent me. It looked like a good one, full of creaky staircases and skeleton hands. I settled in to read for awhile.

Jill had brought a pile of magazines, and she and Maggie were leafing through them. Sunny was trying out a new shade of fingernail polish, putting it on her toes before she applied it to her fingers. We were pretty quiet for an hour or so.

"Hey, where did everybody go?" Sunny asked suddenly. "The beach really emptied out."

I looked up. She was right — hardly anyone was on the beach except for us. The surfers had left, and not many people were sitting or strolling on the sand. "The fog is coming in," I said, peering out toward the ocean. "I guess that's why they took off early."

"It's kind of creepy," said Jill. "I wish Liz were coming back for us sooner."

"I don't think it's so creepy," said Maggie. "I like the fog. It's like a big blanket, covering the beach."

I didn't say anything, but I agreed with Jill. I was beginning to feel creeped out. It was about four-thirty, and the sun was starting to go down as the fog rolled in. "Maybe we should start packing up," I said. "We could wait for Liz in the parking lot."

"Good idea," agreed Sunny. "It's turning

kind of chilly out here." I could tell she didn't want to admit to being spooked any more than I did. She stood up and started to shake out her blanket. I began to toss things into my beach bag, making sure I didn't forget anything. If you leave a hairbrush or a sneaker on the beach, it's hard to find.

Jill was folding up her blanket and Maggie was brushing the sand off her feet. I was just tucking the ghost story book into my bag when I heard Sunny gasp. "There's still a surfer out there!" she said. "I don't believe it. It's almost dark!"

"The surfer ghost," I whispered, peering at the waves. "It must be him."

"I don't see anybody," said Jill, squinting.

"Right there," said Sunny, pointing.

"All the way out there?" replied Maggie. "But that's so far out. I can hardly see."

We strained our eyes, trying to catch sight of the surfer. "He's a little closer now," said Sunny. "I can see him better. And I don't think it's Thrash, Dawn — or Thrash's ghost. He has pretty short hair, for one thing."

"He's coming in toward the old pier!" cried Maggie. "Let's run down there and see if we can get a better look."

We dropped our stuff on the sand and started to run, keeping an eye on the surfer. "Whoa!" said Sunny, all of a sudden. She stopped short. "Did you see that?"

"What?" I asked.

"That guy just did an aerial. A three-sixty!"

"Wow!" I exclaimed. Aerial maneuvers are really hard. You perform them when your surfboard is totally in the air while you're turning. And a three-sixty is the hardest turn to make, because you spin all the way around until you're facing the direction in which you started.

"Nobody on this beach can surf like that," said Sunny slowly. "In fact, I've only seen one person do that move." She gave me a serious look. "Thrash," she said. "I saw Thrash do that, about a month ago."

Jill and Maggie were staring at Sunny, and so was I. "You mean — " I started to say.

"I mean, short hair or not, that surfer *must* be Thrash. Or Thrash's ghost. I still don't think there's any such thing as a real ghost, but I know I saw *something* strange out there."

"Well, we've lost him now, whoever he is," spoke up Jill. "I can't see him anymore." She looked again at the waves, and shook her head. "Anyway, we should get moving if we're going to meet Liz on time."

It was nearly dark as we walked back to our spot and picked up our stuff. Jill and Maggie grabbed their things and walked on ahead, but Sunny and I lagged behind, still glancing at the waves. "You know," said Sunny. "Whether or not that was an actual ghost, I'm beginning to think there *is* something fishy going on at the beach. I'm going to help you investigate. From now on, we're a team."

I stuck out my hand, and we slapped each other five. "All right, partner," I said.

On the way to the parking lot, we passed the concession stand. It was almost closing time, and the workers were cleaning up. A couple of them were kids I know, and I waved. Then I noticed a new guy. He had short black hair and a deep tan, and I know this sounds silly, but he gave me the creeps. I stared at him for a second, and then I looked away and dashed after my friends. Within minutes, we were piling into Liz's beat-up car. I was surprised at how relieved I felt as we drove off. I was glad to be safe in a car, heading away from the beach on that foggy, dark night.

CHAPTER 10

Wednesday

Dear Shannon,
  I sure wish you and the other BSC members could be here to help me solve this mystery. I can't seem to get anywhere with it! I haven't found any new clues in days, and meanwhile things are getting dangerous on the beach. I always thought of the beach as a safe and beautiful place, but lately I'm not so sure about that...

Around the time I wrote that letter to Shannon, I was feeling pretty frustrated with my mystery. The can of wax had been the last clue, and finding that seemed like a long time ago. Sunny was helping me now, and I was glad to have her company, but even with two of us working we couldn't seem to get anywhere. I'd returned to my surfing lessons, but Sunny and I made time to talk to people on the beach every day, hoping to find someone who had witnessed Thrash's fatal accident. Nobody had seen anything. We checked with the police on a regular basis. The only thing that happened was that they got sick of seeing us walk into the station. And we combed the beach, looking for any sign of Thrash, but we never found a thing.

Sometimes I felt ready to give up, but Sunny would convince me that we needed to continue working. Other times, Sunny would say there was no point in trying to solve the mystery, but I would talk her into one more round of questions or one more walk down the beach.

What really kept us going was our sense that the beach was becoming a dangerous place. I don't know if it was because Thrash's ghost was wreaking vengeance (lots of people talked about that) or if it was just coincidence, but in the week or so after Sunny, Jill, Maggie, and I saw the surfer ghost, there were a lot of accidents on the beach. And they didn't happen just to surfers.

For example, one day at the children's program, the kids were playing Simon Says. Dean was Simon, and he was doing all kinds of funny things. The kids were giggling as they tried to keep up with him. "Simon says rub your belly with one hand while you pat the top of your head with the other," Dean would say. "Simon says try to kiss your elbow." Then he'd catch them up by saying, "Do the moon walk," while he demonstrated a perfect move. Before long, only four kids were left. Ruby, the girl who rides on our bus, was one of them.

"Simon says walk like a penguin," said Dean, showing them how to waddle along in the sand. Suddenly, I heard a shriek that sounded serious. Ruby sat down in the sand, holding her left foot and wailing like a fire engine. I rushed to her side.

"What happened?" I asked, reaching for her foot. I saw a ragged cut on it, and a small amount of blood. Fortunately, the cut wasn't deep, but it looked like it must hurt a lot.

"I stepped on something," sobbed Ruby. "Something awful!"

While Alyssa cleaned and bandaged the cut,

Sunny and I combed the sand where she had been penguin-walking. We couldn't find anything that might have cut Ruby's foot.

The next day, Ruby was back in high spirits. She said her foot hardly hurt at all, and that her mom had given her chocolate pudding as a special treat the night before. That day, everything went smoothly at the children's program. But after our surfing lesson, when Sunny and I were packing up to leave the beach, we heard sirens. We ran to the parking area to see what had happened, and found a small fire engine and an ambulance pulled up by the concession stand.

"What happened?" Sunny asked one of the workers.

"Freak accident," said the boy. "The grill flared up all of a sudden and burned Brenda's eyebrows right off! Luckily, she wasn't hurt aside from that. The ambulance guys just checked her out, and she's fine."

We saw the firemen examining the grill and shaking their heads as if they couldn't figure out what was wrong with it. And, as far as we heard in the days after the accident, they never *could* explain the flare-up.

A couple of days later, a man returned to the parking lot to get his car and found that all four tires had gone flat, for no apparent reason. Another man said he had been dive-bombed by an angry seagull. And a woman was stung by a jellyfish while she was walking in the shallow water at the edge of the beach.

Sunny and I tried to make light of each incident, but even though nobody had been seriously hurt, we were scared. Why were all these things happening at once? I mean, I knew that these accidents could happen at any beach, but all in the space of a week? It was seriously weird. We took extra care when we watched the kids at the beach program, making sure none of them went unsupervised for even a few minutes. And Sunny and I stuck together like glue. "I'll watch out for you if you'll watch out for me," she joked.

I felt most nervous while I was surfing. I still loved it, and I looked forward to my lessons. But accidents were happening to surfers, too. In fact, there had been at least one accident every day for awhile. As I've said, surfing *can* be a dangerous sport, and there is always the potential for trouble when you're out in the water. Waves are not entirely predictable, and even the best surfers can make bad judgments.

But bad judgment didn't seem to be the problem. Bad *luck* did — and lots of good surfers were having it. Paul was hurt when he fell off his board and it was carried toward him by a wave. It hit him on the shoulder, and since then his arm has been in a sling.

Wanda wiped out and was underwater for so long she almost drowned. And somebody else banged into the old pilings where the pier used to be. Rosemary was caught in the riptide (that's a strong current that moves away from shore) and the lifeguards had to go after her in their rubber boat.

T.J. wiped out when his board didn't respond the way it should have during a turn he was trying to make. Then the same thing happened to somebody else. And that's when the rumors started.

"No way were the waves that gnarly," said Carter one day when Sunny and I were making our usual rounds, talking to the surfers. "I mean, those dudes can handle massive screamers, and those rollers weren't anywhere near overhead."

"So what are you saying?" asked Sunny.

"I'm saying that somebody messed with their boards. Just like somebody messed with Paul's leash."

"What?" I said. I hadn't heard anything about Paul's leash. (A leash is a cord that connects at one end to a surfboard and at the other to a band around the surfer's ankle. It keeps the board from getting lost, and sometimes helps to guard against the board hitting the surfer if he falls off.)

"Truth, man," said Carter. "Everybody's talking about it. They're saying that some wack wants to win that competition real bad. So bad he doesn't care if another dude gets hurt. So bad he might mess with a board. Some of the dudes are getting pretty nervous about it. I heard Spanky dropped out of the competition."

"He *did*?" I asked. I was surprised. Spanky is a great surfer, and everybody thought he'd do well in the competition.

"Sure," replied Carter. "I mean, Thrash is history, right? Spanky isn't interested in getting killed, too. So he's going down to Mexico for awhile, to surf where he won't get hurt."

The rumors kept flying, and the accidents kept happening. But Sunny and I continued to surf. You might think we were crazy, but we weren't ready to give up our new sport. Besides, the *good*, experienced surfers were getting hurt, not the grommets like us. We were no threat in the competition. Therefore, nobody was going to try to get rid of us. Right? Well, the theory made sense to us. Anyway, Buck said we were really coming along, and that if we stopped practicing now we would never improve.

Then, one afternoon (it was the day after I wrote that letter to Shannon, as a matter of fact), something terrible happened. Sunny and

I had just finished our lesson, and we were standing on the beach with our surfboards. "I'm exhausted," I said. "Ready to start packing up?"

"In a few minutes," said Sunny. "I want to go out one more time. Look at those waves! They're perfect." She had a point. It had been a great afternoon, and the waves were still rolling in regularly, looking green and glassy. They were just the right height, too. Five or six people were paddling out on their boards, getting ready to ride back in.

"You're right," I agreed. For a second, I thought about going back in with Sunny. But then I felt a wave of tiredness roll over me, and I knew I shouldn't. Buck says it's dangerous to surf when you're not feeling your strongest. "You go ahead," I said. "I'll watch and give you a report on your form."

Sunny grinned. "You better give me high marks," she said. She tossed her hair back, grabbed her board, and ran into the water. She put the board down, lay on top of it, and started to paddle out. When she reached the spot where the other surfers were waiting, she turned and watched the rollers coming in. In turn, each of the surfers caught one. It's bad surfing manners to take somebody else's wave, so Sunny waited patiently until everybody else was already riding in. Then she got ready for the next wave. When it came, she turned her board toward shore, and as the wave rushed along, she climbed onto it and began to ride.

"Looking good!" I called, even though I knew there was no way she could hear me over the booming surf. Sunny stood with her arms out, balancing carefully. Even from a distance, I could tell she wore a big smile on her face.

And then, Sunny disappeared. "Oh, my lord!" I cried, as soon as I saw that she was down. I ran to the edge of the water and scanned the waves, waiting for her head to pop up. It seemed like hours until I saw first her board, and then her head and shoulders, riding in toward shore on a gentle wave. I ran to meet her and helped her out of the water and onto the sand. She was gasping for breath and coughing.

"Are you okay?" I asked. "What happened?"

"Don't know," she said, still coughing. "I think the nose went under."

I knew just what she was talking about. Once the nose goes under the water, there's almost no way to keep from falling off your board.

"My elbow is killing me," said Sunny. "And my shoulder, too. I really got tossed around."

By that time a crowd had gathered, and one of the lifeguards was checking Sunny for broken bones. "Looks like you'll survive," he said, "but you better head to the hospital and get a real exam."

Sunny spent that night at the hospital. She was bruised badly, and the doctors wanted to keep her for observation. Her mother called me the next morning and told me she'd asked Sunny to quit surfing, at least for a few weeks. "But that means she can't be in the competition," I said.

"That's right," replied her mother. "And she's very disappointed about it. But she asked me to tell you not to give up. And she said not to give up on 'the other thing,' either. Whatever that means."

I didn't tell Mrs. Winslow, but I knew exactly what Sunny meant. "The other thing" was our mystery, of course. Now it was more important than ever to get to the bottom of it.

CHAPTER 11

Saturday

Dear Dawn,

Your mystery sounds so cool! I wish
I could be there to help you to investigate (and maybe get in some surfing,
too!). Meanwhile, back in Stoneybrook,
things haven't changed too much.
Except for one thing. I know you've
heard about the Arnold twins and
what they're going through. Well, things
got even worse before they got better.
But I think Marilyn and Carolyn are
on the right track now....

That was only part of a long letter that Stacey sent me, explaining the Marilyn-and-Carolyn situation in detail. Basically, the twins had been stuck together like glue, and it had been driving everybody in the BSC crazy. Especially Stacey, who had been sitting for them more than anybody else.

During the week before she wrote to me, she sat for them three times. On Sunday, she was at their house in the afternoon. Mr. and Mrs. Arnold had gone to the christening of a friend's baby, leaving the twins with strict instructions about their chores. They were both to clean their rooms, Marilyn was supposed to load the dishwasher, and Carolyn was supposed to dust the furniture in the living room.

Stacey was glad to see that Carolyn was feeling a lot better. Her ankle had healed, and she didn't have to wear the ace bandage anymore. Her crutches were propped by the front door, waiting for Mr. Arnold to return them to the hospital the next day. Stacey was relieved. She figured the twins would be back to normal, and that Marilyn would feel all right about letting Carolyn out of her sight. But Stacey was wrong. Marilyn was still taking her promise very seriously. The twins were inseparable.

Stacey had hoped that she and the twins could have some fun once the girls finished their chores, but their chores filled up the whole afternoon. Why? Because neither of them could or would do anything alone. Marilyn had to watch while Carolyn vacuumed her room. Marilyn made sure Carolyn was close by while *she* cleaned *her* room. (Which wasn't too messy, since Marilyn was still sleeping in her sister's room.) After that, they both headed for the kitchen, where Carolyn hovered around while Marilyn loaded the dishwasher. Then they went to the living room, and Marilyn watched Carolyn dust. Stacey was exasperated, to say the least.

On Tuesday, Stacey met the twins after school and spent the afternoon with them. They were both doing gymnastics in the basement again, now that Carolyn was well. But they were being very careful. Very, *very* careful. Marilyn watched every single step that Carolyn took, even when she wasn't doing anything dangerous. And Carolyn was equally zealous about watching Marilyn. "It was like ultra-ultra spotting," Stacey wrote me. "I mean, Carolyn couldn't take a *breath* without Marilyn trying to help her. Ridiculous!"

On Thursday, Stacey saw the same pattern. The twins were never out of each other's sight.

They were driving Stacey crazy, and she knew she had to do something about it. But what? She thought about it all night Thursday and all day Friday, but she couldn't come up with a solution. She had another job booked at the Arnolds' on Saturday afternoon, and she was dying to figure something out before then. Finally, at Friday's BSC meeting, she told the others what was happening.

"It can't be healthy for them to be together all the time like that," said Mary Anne. "I mean, especially since they're twins. They need their separate identities."

"I know," replied Stacey. "That's exactly the problem. And I have a feeling that Mr. and Mrs. Arnold think so, too. They seem a little impatient with the twins."

"They'd probably be grateful if we could help," mused Kristy.

My friends thought about the problem for awhile, but nobody came up with any suggestions. And then the phone began to ring, and they were busy setting up jobs.

By the time the phone stopped ringing, it was almost six o'clock. "Phew!" said Shannon, hanging up after the last call. "We're booked solid for the next week."

Mary Anne looked at the record book. "No kidding," she said. "If anybody else calls, we're going to have a problem. I mean, every single one of us has a job tomorrow afternoon!"

Stacey had been deep in thought while the others were booking jobs. But Mary Anne's comment seemed to wake her up. "That's it!" she cried. She grabbed a pencil and a piece of paper from Claudia's desk. "Okay, who's sitting where tomorrow afternoon?"

"I'll be at the Pikes'," said Kristy. "Mal and I will be sitting together. We're going to do quiet, indoor activities." That was the deal the Pikes had made with Mal. While she was recovering from mono, she could sit for her own brothers and sisters with another club member, as long as she stayed inside.

"Great," said Stacey, scribbling notes.

"I have a job at the Papadakises'," said Shannon.

Claudia was taking Charlotte Johanssen to the art museum, and Mary Anne would be bringing Logan's brother and sister to watch one of his basketball games.

"I'll be at the Braddocks'," added Jessi. "But why are you asking?"

"I have a plan!" said Stacey, her eyes gleaming. "Ready for this?" She leaned forward and told them her idea.

The next day, Stacey headed for the Arnolds', feeling much more optimistic. She was almost positive that her plan would work.

Mrs. Arnold answered the door when Stacey knocked. "Oh, I'm glad to see you!" she said. "Am I ever ready for a break from the twins." She laughed and shook her head. "I know it's just a phase, but I sure hope they'll get over it soon."

"I know what you mean," replied Stacey.

"The girls are downstairs," said Mrs. Arnold. "They're working on a new gymnastics routine in which they can perform at the same time. They call it 'twin-nastics.' "

Stacey laughed. "Great name," she said. "Maybe it'll be an Olympic event someday."

"Hi, you guys!" she said, as she ran down the stairs.

"Hi, Stacey!" said Marilyn.

"Want to see our new routine?" asked Carolyn.

"Sure," said Stacey. She sat on the bottom step and watched as they performed. As she explained in her letter, they had worked out their routine very neatly. One twin would be on the balance beam, for example, and the other would be spotting her but also performing similar moves, on the floor. "Looks great, girls," said Stacey. "What does your gymnastics teacher think of this?"

"She hasn't seen it yet," said Carolyn.

"We just started to work on it," explained Marilyn. "But I'm — *we're* — sure she'll like it."

Stacey nodded. The girls returned to their practicing, and Stacey played audience. Once in awhile she sneaked a glance at her watch. At precisely two o'clock, the phone rang. "All *right!*" Stacey said under her breath. She ran upstairs to answer it. It was Kristy, as she had known it would be. The plan was in motion.

"Hi, Stacey," said Kristy. "I'm at the Pikes', and I brought over the new Flying Horses tape. Margo wants to know if Marilyn would like to hear it, too."

Good. Kristy was sticking to the script. "Hold on," said Stacey. "I'll get Marilyn." She called down the stairs, and both girls came running up.

Marilyn got on the phone. "Hello?" she said. Kristy had put Margo on the other end, and Margo repeated her invitation. Marilyn listened, and broke into a smile. "I'd *love* to hear it," she said. Then she caught herself. "I mean — if *Carolyn* can come, too. She listened again, and frowned. Then she looked up at Stacey. "Margo is only allowed to invite one person over today," she said.

"So. You can go by yourself."

Marilyn shook her head. "No, I can't," she said reluctantly. "Sorry, Margo, but I guess I can't come." She hung up and shrugged. "Oh, well," she said. She and Carolyn headed back to the basement.

Stacey followed them, checking her watch again. At exactly two-fifteen, the phone rang again. This time, it was Jessi, calling from the Braddocks'. Haley wanted Carolyn to come play with her new video game. When Carolyn got on the phone, a grin spread across her face. "Princess Power?" she squealed. "I've been *dying* to play that!" She paused. "Can Marilyn come, too?"

Haley said the game was meant for only two players. Carolyn looked hopefully at Marilyn, but Marilyn shook her head, and Carolyn had to say no to Haley.

The girls, downcast, trudged back to the basement. Stacey stood in the kitchen, timing them. Exactly seven minutes later, Marilyn and Carolyn pounded back up the stairs.

"We changed our minds!" exclaimed Carolyn.

"We decided it was okay to be apart — for a couple of hours, anyway," said Marilyn.

Carolyn called Haley, and Marilyn called Margo, and soon they were ready to go. The girls decided they would all walk to the Pikes' first, and then Stacey and Carolyn would continue to the Braddocks'. Stacey wrote Mrs. Arnold a note, explaining where they had gone, and then they were off.

Stacey smiled to herself as she and the twins headed down the sidewalk. "I knew it was only a little step," she wrote to me that night, "but it *was* a step. That's good enough for me."

CHAPTER 12

Thursday

Dear Mary Anne,

Stacey wrote me about the latest development with the Arnold twins. Reading her letter sure made me miss the BSC. The We ♥ Kids Club is great, but they're not quite as involved with their clients as the BSC is. I miss those meetings when we would sit around and talk, talk, talk about what was going on with the kids.

Meanwhile, things are really heating up around here. Today I got my first big break in the mystery. Here's how it happened....

I wrote that letter to Mary Anne one night after a long — and exciting — afternoon at the beach. I was there for the kids' program, but I wasn't working with Sunny or Alyssa. I had a special assignment: a one-on-one sitting job with Stephie Robertson. See, the beach program was involved in rehearsing for this play to be put on for the parents. It was a special production of *Alice in Wonderland*, which Alyssa and Sondra had adapted so that it took place on a beach. It was called *Alice at the Beach*, and the kids were having a great time with it. But Stephie is incredibly shy. She didn't want to be in the play, and Alyssa didn't want to force her. Instead, Alyssa had arranged for Stephie to be my responsibility during rehearsal times.

We had been enjoying our time together, Stephie and I. She's a great kid. In fact, she reminds me more than a little bit of Mary Anne, and it's not just because they're both so shy. It's also because, like Mary Anne, Stephie is an only child. And she's growing up without a mother, just the way Mary Anne did. Stephie's mom died when Stephie was just a baby. Her dad has raised her, and I know he tries hard, just as Mary Anne's dad always did, but it's not always easy for a man to raise a daughter by himself. He has help —

a nannie lives with them — but I can tell that Stephie misses having a mom. She doesn't talk about it, but I can just tell anyway, maybe because I'm so close to Mary Anne.

Anyway, Stephie and I had found plenty to do. We took long walks, exploring parts of the beach we'd never been to before. We watched the surfers, and rated their form. And we spent a lot of time collecting pebbles, beach glass, and shells.

Stephie's dad had given her a nature guide to beaches, and we had been working our way through it. We had identified all the birds we saw, and most of the shells we had picked up. We had even learned a lot about different kinds of seaweed! Those afternoons with Stephie were great. The time I spent with her was relaxing, and I needed to relax. Most of the time I was caught up in trying to solve the mystery of Thrash's disappearance, but when I was with Stephie I managed to put that aside. Instead of thinking about mutilated surfboards and phantom surfers, I concentrated on being a friend to Stephie.

That Thursday, the day I wrote the letter to Mary Anne, Stephie and I had been busy categorizing the pebbles we had collected. We'd made different piles for green rocks, black rocks, rocks with stripes, white rocks — well, you get the picture. There was even a pile for heart-shaped rocks, which were Stephie's favorites. I liked the flat rocks best, the ones you could use for skipping stones.

We had also spent some time reading to each other. Stephie loves books, and she's an excellent reader. I bet she'd get along great with Charlotte Johanssen. Stephie's been working her way through the Narnia books, and we were in the middle of *The Silver Chair* that day. As Stephie read, I lay back in the sand and watched the waves roll in. A lot of surfers were out that afternoon; the competition was the following weekend, and everybody was getting in their practice time.

When Stephie finished her chapter, I stretched and sat up. "I'm hungry," I said. "How about you?"

"I'm starved," she replied, smiling.

"Let's go get smoothies," I suggested. Smoothies are blended fruit drinks made with yogurt, and they are delicious. My favorite kind is banana-strawberry. The concession stand at the beach makes them with tons of fresh fruit.

"All *right!*" said Stephie. "I want a peach one today."

We packed up our stuff and headed to the concession stand. On the way, Stephie and I waved to Sunny and some of the kids in the beach program, who were rehearsing a scene in which Alice meets the surfing Cheshire Cat.

"They look like they're having a good time," I said to Stephie. I wondered if she felt left out.

"I'm having a good time, too," she said, taking my hand and looking up at me with a smile.

The concession stand was crowded with people waiting to order fries, hot dogs, and smoothies. Stephie and I got in line, and I craned my neck, curious to see who was working that day. A girl named Shari was running the blender, but none of the other people looked familiar. Then I saw him. That new guy, the one with the black hair. The one who had given me the creeps the first time I saw him. He *still* gave me the creeps, but I couldn't figure out why. He was working the grill, flipping burgers a mile a minute. As the line we stood in edged forward, I stared hard at the guy, trying to figure it out. He wasn't being rude to the customers, or staring at girls or anything. He was just doing his job.

The closer I moved to the counter, the better I could see him. He was dressed like the other workers, in cut-offs and a T-shirt. His hair was very short, practically a buzzcut. He must have gotten the haircut recently, too, because his neck wasn't as tan as the rest of him. Unlike the rest of the workers, who were wearing wild jewelry, he wore none. I did notice, though, that he had holes in his ears for pierced earrings. Two on the left, and three on the right. I counted.

He was wearing dark, dark sunglasses, the kind that wrap around your head and make you look like some kind of space ranger. And as he turned to lay a burger on a bun, I noticed a funny white mark on his finger. A scar? I tried to get a closer look, but just then I realized that the girl behind the counter was talking to me. It was my turn to be served, and Shari was waiting on me.

"Hey, Dawn," she said. "I bet you're here for a smoothie. Strawberry-banana, right?"

I nodded. "Right," I said. "I guess I'm pretty predictable, huh?"

"Oh, we just get to know all the regular orders," she said. "Anything else?"

I ordered a peach smoothie for Stephie, and we watched while Shari blended our drinks for us.

"Yum!" said Stephie, as Shari dumped sliced peaches into the blender. Her drink was ready first, and she started sipping it while Shari fixed mine.

"All set?" asked Shari, setting my drink on the counter. I nodded, and handed her some money. As she was making my change, I glanced once more at the creepy guy. Suddenly, I realized something incredible. Something so wild, I could hardly believe it. "Dawn?" asked Shari, holding out my change. "What's the matter? You look like you saw a ghost or something."

I tried to laugh. "I'm okay," I said. I took the change, grabbed my smoothie, and thanked her. "Let's go, Stephie," I said.

We left the concession stand and walked toward the parking lot, since it was almost time to catch the bus home. "What happened?" asked Stephie. "You look upset."

"It's nothing," I said. I wasn't ready to tell *anybody* what I had figured out. Stephie and I sipped our smoothies while we waited for the bus. I could hardly taste mine, but I pretended it was delicious. I chatted with Stephie about our plans for the next day, but I wasn't paying much attention to what she said.

When Sunny met us in the parking lot, I asked if I could come over to her house after we got home. "I have something to tell you," I said. "Something about — *you* know."

Her eyes widened, and she gave me a curious look. I shook my head, letting her know that I couldn't talk about it until we were alone. We boarded the bus soon after that, and I felt relieved to sit back in my seat and listen to the kids' songs and tease each other.

When I got home, I ran to my room and

dumped my beach stuff. Then I headed for Sunny's. She let me in, and we ran to her room and closed the door.

"You'll never believe who I saw today," I said.

"Who?" she asked.

"It was at the concession stand. This new guy there gives me the creeps for some reason. I've tried and tried to figure out why, but I couldn't. And then, suddenly, I knew who he was."

"*Who?*" Sunny asked again.

"Thrash."

"You're kidding."

"Nope. It was him. He looks different, but I know he's Thrash. It's like he's in disguise." I described the guy to Sunny, and then I explained how I had figured out he was Thrash. "The mark on his finger tipped me off," I said. "It's a tan line around the ring he used to wear. The one that's shaped like a snake?"

"Are you *sure*?" Sunny asked.

I nodded. "He cut off his hair and dyed what was left," I said. "That's why his neck is kind of pale — because his hair used to be longer. And I remember how many holes he had for pierced earrings, because it's one more than I have."

Sunny looked stunned. "But if he *is* Thrash — " she began.

"He isn't dead," I finished. "But he's still hanging around the beach. Why? What's he up to?"

"This is wild," said Sunny. "Maybe we should tell the police."

"No way," I said. "For one thing, they wouldn't believe us, just because this *is* so wild. And for another, they don't seem to care what happened to him. I think we have to check this out on our own."

Before long, I had talked Sunny into seeing things my way. We spent half an hour planning what to do next, and then I went home for dinner. My head was spinning. Thrash wasn't dead, after all. He was very much alive. Alive and well and working — undercover — at the concession stand.

CHAPTER 13

Friday

Dear Claudia,
   The mystery of the surfer ghost just keeps growing. Mary Anne probably told you how I learned that Thrash is still alive. Once I discovered that, all I had to do was find out what he was doing hanging around the beach in disguise. This mystery sure is keeping me busy!

"Check it out, Sunny," I whispered, nudging her. It was the day after I had spotted Thrash, and Sunny and I had wasted no time putting our plan into action. We had finished up at the beach program, and raced to the concession stand to see if Thrash would be there again. I saw him right away. He was cutting up lettuce for sandwiches, and he seemed to be concentrating hard on his work. I took the opportunity to point him out to Sunny.

No way!" she whispered. "Are you *sure* that's him?"

Just then, Thrash turned toward the counter, and Sunny got a good look at him. He was still wearing sunglasses, but I knew she was checking out his pierced-earring holes and the strange tan line on his finger. "Hmmm," she said. "You know, I think you're right. But what is he doing *here*?"

"That's what we have to find out," I whispered. I stepped up to the counter and ordered us each a smoothie. We watched Thrash carefully while we were waiting to be served, and then we walked down the beach, sipping our drinks. We decided to watch Thrash as much as possible and try to figure out what he was up to. Since Sunny still couldn't surf, she could spy on him while I took my lessons and practiced. And since I was still sitting for Stephie during the hours of the beach program, I would try to hang around the concession stand and watch him then. We figured we might be able to find out why he was still at the beach.

Over the next few days, we spied all the time. One or the other of us kept an eye on Thrash whenever we were at the beach. But we didn't find out much. Basically, all he did was work. Sometimes he worked the grill, flipping burgers and cooking hot dogs. Sometimes he ran the blender, making smoothies. And sometimes he made french fries. But he never went surfing, never did anything out of the ordinary. I have to admit that Sunny and I were both feeling frustrated.

Meanwhile, I was practicing hard for the surfing competition. I was even having trouble concentrating on my schoolwork, because I was so focused on the competition. Buck said he was proud of my progress, and that I was turning into a "radical surfer." I knew he was exaggerating to make me feel more confident, but I knew I really *was* improving. Some days I felt so in tune with the waves that it seemed I had been born in the water. I knew I wouldn't win any major prizes in the competition, but I was looking forward to it anyway. I was especially excited about watching the best surfers do their stuff.

There were still reports, now and then, of sightings of the surfer ghost. Since Sunny and I were never at the beach after dark, we didn't see him. But everybody was talking about the amazing moves the ghost could pull. They joked about the ghost entering the competition, saying he could probably win first prize if he did.

Sunny and I checked with the police a couple of times, but they had no new leads on the case. They still thought Thrash was either dead or missing, and they weren't exactly hot on the trail. In fact, they seemed to have written him off and moved on to other things.

The day of the competition grew closer and closer. All the surfers were practicing hard, and some were riding the waves from early morning until the sun went down. Certain surfers were beginning to look discouraged, and others were wearing this confident, almost cocky look. There was a lot of talk on the beach about who would win what prize. Surfers like Gonzo and T.J. seemed to regard each other suspiciously. They checked out each other's form and copied moves they thought might catch the judges' eyes. Even with Spanky gone, there were plenty of really excellent surfers getting ready to compete.

On Saturday, the day before the competition, Alyssa asked Sunny to stay for an extra half hour after the beach program ended. Sunny had agreed weeks ago to help with the sets for the play when the time came, and now, said Alyssa, the time had come. I was on my own until my lesson started, so of course I headed for the concession stand to check up on Thrash. Guess what? He wasn't there. He wasn't making burgers, or frying fries, or blending smoothies. I hung around for a few minutes, hoping he was just on a break and would turn up soon. But there was no sign of him. Finally, I stepped up to the counter and ordered a smoothie. When the girl who made it handed it over, I spoke up. "Hey, where's that other guy that usually works here?" I asked casually. "You know, the one with the short hair."

The girl shrugged. "I think he asked for the day off. Why?"

I thought fast. "Oh, he loaned me fifteen cents the other day when I didn't have enough change," I said, trying to sound convincing. "I wanted to pay him back."

She nodded. "He'll probably be here tomorrow," she said. "Anyway, it's only fifteen cents. I doubt he's worried about it."

I agreed. As I walked away from the stand,

I racked my brain. Where could Thrash be? And why had he taken the day off? I had this feeling that something was up. I guess it was what the detectives on TV call a hunch. Somehow I knew it was important that Thrash had taken off from work on the day before the surfing competition.

I walked by the surf shop, deep in thought. As I rounded the corner of the building, I heard a strange noise. I drew back and set my smoothie down in the sand. Carefully, I peeked around the corner. In back of the shop is a shed where the workers stash their surfboards. And somebody was in it. I walked closer, peering into the semi-darkness. That's when I saw Thrash. He was bending over one of the boards and pushing against its fins with some kind of tool.

He was *tampering* with somebody's board!

I drew back again and thought for a second. What Thrash was doing was wrong, and somebody had to stop him. If he messed up that board, its owner could get seriously hurt. I looked around, hoping to see a policeman — or *anybody* who could help. But nobody was there. It was up to me. I took a deep breath and gathered up my courage. Then I walked into the shed, clearing my throat as I approached Thrash.

"Hey!" I said, trying to sound official. Unfortunately, all that came out was a squeak. Thrash didn't pause in what he was doing. He didn't look up, either. "Hey," I said, more loudly. "What do you think you're doing?"

All of a sudden I wondered if I was nuts. Was this guy really Thrash? Or was he somebody else, somebody who might be really angry about being caught tampering with a board. Somebody who might try to hurt me.

This time, he did look up. But he didn't seem angry or upset. He just grinned at me. "Hey, Kelea," he said. "How's it goin'?"

That's when I knew for sure he was Thrash. He's the only person who has ever called me by that name. "Thrash?" I said, uncertainly.

"That's me."

"So you aren't dead."

"Nope. Alive and kickin'."

"And tampering with somebody's board," I said. "That's not right."

"Hey, somebody tried to off me," he replied, defensively. "You know, kill me. Make sure I wasn't in the competition. I know who did it, too. Well, I wiped out pretty bad after he messed with my board, but I sure didn't buy the farm. I let him think I did, though. I want to teach that jerk a lesson."

"What do you mean?"

"Why do you think I'm still hanging around?" he asked. "And why do you think I look like this?" He put down the tool and ran a hand through his short black hair. "I *hated* to cut my hair, man, but it was the only way. I figured if I disguised myself, I could still hang out here. I could keep surfing, and prepare for the competition. I could still win it, too, and make some dough so I can head Down Under, to Australia."

"But I guess you're not so sure you can win honestly," I said, "since you're messing up that board."

He glared at me. "I'd win no matter what. But I want to teach this guy a lesson. Nobody messes with Thrash."

"What if he gets hurt?" I asked.

He shrugged. "Not my problem. I mean, that dude wasn't worried about *me* getting hurt, was he?"

"Have you been messing with other people's boards?" I asked. "I mean, there have been all these accidents, and — "

"I'm not responsible," Thrash said, holding up his hand as if he were swearing to it. "This is the only one I care about. I just want to get that guy back for what he did to me."

I decided to change the subject while I thought about what to do next. I had to prevent Thrash from tampering with that board.

"You said you've been surfing, but I've never seen you out there."

"Never seen the Surfer Ghost?" he said, grinning.

"You mean — ?" I began. My mouth dropped open.

He nodded. "That's me. I've been riding the waves by moonlight, just to make sure nobody tries to spy on me and steal my moves." He laughed. "It's a riot how they all think I'm a spook," he added.

"I saw you," I said. "You really did look like a ghost out there."

"Cool." He picked up his tool again and bent over the board.

"Don't do it," I said. "Please? I mean, I understand that you want revenge, but two wrongs don't make a right." I didn't *mean* to sound like a teacher; the words just popped out. "And anyway, you said you could win the competition without messing up that guy's board. I think you should enter the competition honestly, under your own name. That way, you can prove to everyone that you really are the best surfer."

Thrash gave me a long look. "Yeah, but if I just turn up alive, the guy who messed up my board is going to get away with it. What about that?"

"There has to be a way to make sure he gets

in trouble for what he did," I said. "Let me think for a second." I leaned against a saw-horse.

Thrash stood there looking at me. "You're too much, Kelea," he said. " Why do you want to help a bum like me, anyway?"

I didn't know how to answer him, because it was a mystery to me, too. But there was something I liked about Thrash. He was a ter-rific surfer, and I knew he deserved a chance to win that competition fair and square. And I knew that the guy who had messed with his board deserved some kind of punishment for what he had done. Just then, I had a great idea. I smiled at him. "I don't know *why*, Thrash," I said. "But I think I know *how*."

CHAPTER 14

Sunday

Dear Kristy,
   Wow! How can I begin to
tell you about everything
that happened today? I'm
totally exhausted, and totally
stuffed with artichokes and
vegetarian lasagna (Dad
took us out to dinner after
the contest) but I'll try to
stay awake long enough to
write down the main events
of the day. So, let's see. First
of all, I woke up late...

"Oh, no!" I sat bolt upright in bed that morning, staring at the clock. I was going to have to *hustle* if I wanted to arrive at the beach on time. I checked the alarm, sure something was wrong with it. Why hadn't it gone off? I was *positive* I had set it when I went to bed the night before. Then my glance fell on a pink sheet of paper Buck had handed me the day before, after my last lesson. "Preparation for Competition," it said at the top. It listed the things you should do before a contest, and at the top of the list was, "Be sure to get plenty of rest the night before you compete." Well, I had definitely done that!

I jumped up and started to gather my stuff together. As I was throwing things into my beach bag, I heard a soft knock on the door. "Sunshine?" asked Dad, coming into my room. "Feeling okay? Ready to show the judges your stuff?"

I grinned. "As ready as I'll ever be. That is, if I can get there on time."

"Don't worry about *that*," he said. "I'll get you there. Carol arrived ten minutes ago, and she and Jeff are ready to head out whenever you are." He gave me a big hug. "We're so excited about watching you compete," he said.

"Oh, Dad. Really, I'm not very good yet. I hope you're not expecting too much."

He just hugged me again. "Come on down when you're ready," he said.

When I got downstairs, they were waiting for me: Dad, Carol, and Jeff. "Let's go!" I said.

Carol handed me a bagel from the breakfast table. "You can't compete on an empty stomach," she said with a smile.

"Thanks," I replied, thinking that Carol had been pretty easy to get along with lately. She was right, too. "Make sure to eat something" was the *second* item on Buck's list. I didn't feel hungry at all — I was jittery and excited. But I took a bite of the bagel anyway, and brought it and an orange with me to the car.

We piled in, Jeff sitting beside me in the back seat, and soon we were on our way. As we drove, Dad kept up a steady stream of talk about what a perfect day it was for the contest, and how crowded the beach would be for the big event. I just sat, looking out the window, thinking over everything I had learned from Buck. I thought about how to choose the right wave, and how to sense the moment to climb up and ride it. I reviewed my best rides, picturing the things I had done right. "Positive visualization," Buck calls it. He says the pros do it. In the middle of one of my "rides," I felt Jeff's elbow digging into my side.

"This is for you," he said. "For today. I'm lending it to you, for good luck." He handed me a penny. "I found it in school one day," he said. "And I kept it. It's a lucky penny."

"Thanks, Jeff," I said, putting my arm around him and giving him a squeeze. "I'll put it in my wetsuit pocket." I tucked it away. Then I looked out the window again. We were nearing the beach, and I started to think about Thrash, wondering what he would do about competing. He had told me, at the end of our talk, that he was going to go to the police and tell them everything he knew about the guy who had tampered with his board. I was glad, since that was the plan I had come up with. But beyond that, I had no idea what he was doing. For all I knew, he wouldn't show up at the competition. The police might even have put him in jail when he confessed to trying to tamper with the guy's board. Or maybe they had just told him to clear out, leave town. I might never see Thrash again.

Still, I was betting that he would turn up at the competition. Thrash loved being the best surfer on the beach. I didn't think he'd pass up the opportunity to prove it to everyone.

"Wow, it's a mob scene!" said Jeff, when we arrived at the beach. *"Everybody's* here."

He was right. The beach was packed with surfers, fans, and judges. Everybody was milling around, waiting for the contest to begin. The waves looked great — smooth and glassy and not too big. *That* was a relief. I had been worried about having to deal with huge grinders or choppy seas.

"We'll find a spot to sit, Sunshine," said my dad. "Want to leave your stuff with us?"

"I'll take it with me," I said. I was eager to join the group of surfers who were gathering near the judges' stand. "See you later!"

Everyone wished me luck, and I headed toward the group. On the way, I ran into Sunny, who had come to watch the contest even though she couldn't participate. "Good luck!" she said. "And have fun. I'll see you afterward, okay?"

I pointed her in the direction of Dad and Carol and Jeff, and she said she would join them. Then I ran to the judges' stand to check in. As I was giving my name, I heard a murmur run through the crowd of surfers. I looked up just in time to see Thrash stroll to the stand.

He was blond again — I guess he had dyed his hair back — and he was wearing his earrings and the snake ring. He looked as much like his old self as he possibly could. He was even carrying a surfboard like his old one, with black designs on a purple background. I heard a few gasps as he walked through the crowd.

"I'm back from the dead," he announced, with a cocky grin. "And ready to rock and roll."

I heard a strangled scream from behind me, and I turned to see Gonzo drop his surfboard in the sand. Gonzo. I should have known. He had turned completely pale, and he was staring at Thrash as if he were seeing — you guessed it — a ghost. Then he turned, and ran down the beach.

"That's him!" yelled Thrash. "Get him!"

Suddenly, a bunch of men in the crowd, men I hadn't recognized, took off down the beach after Gonzo. They were dressed like surfers, but as soon as they started to chase the guy, I knew — I just *knew* — they were undercover cops.

Sure enough, after they had caught up with Gonzo they pulled badges out of the pockets of their jams. Gonzo immediately confessed to messing with Thrash's board, and the cops took him away. It turned out that the police had talked Thrash into working with them, which was exactly what I had hoped they would do. I knew if he felt the cops were on his side, he would be more likely to enter the competition honestly.

It took awhile for things to calm down, but before long the judges were announcing the start of the competition. The first group to compete would be the beginners. That was me. Suddenly, I felt like running back to Dad and climbing into his lap.

"Go for it, Kelea," said Thrash from behind me. "You can do it."

I smiled at him. "Thanks," I said. "I'll do my best."

The male beginners went first. I watched as one after another of them chose bad waves and wiped out, or took short, unimpressive rides. I started to feel a little better. I might be a beginner, but I was sure I could do better than *that*. I watched the waves carefully, trying to decide which ones I would pick if I were out there.

Finally, the men's division finished and the women's began. There were five of us. We paddled out and began to eye the waves more closely. I was supposed to go second. My stomach was in a knot, but I could also feel a certain kind of energy that I knew would help me through my rides.

Contest scoring is based on a lot of things. The length of the ride, for one. The longer you can ride, the more moves you can catch, and the better you look. Another factor is maneuvers, or moves. The judges watch to see how smoothly you do certain things, and whether you take chances on exciting, radical moves. You also get judged on style, and on how well you choose your waves.

As I waited my turn, I tried again to visualize the perfect ride. When the first surfer finished her ride (a very short one), I waited patiently until a wave I liked came along. Then I rode it in, trying hard to remember everything Buck had told me. It wasn't a bad ride.

Each of us in the division took three turns. My second ride was terrible: I wiped out almost directly in front of the judges' stand. But I stood up and shook the water out of my hair and paddled back out. My third ride was one of the best I've ever had.

After my division was finished, all I could do was watch the other surfers and wait to find out the results. The judges wouldn't announce the winners until the entire competition was over, and at first I didn't know how I could stand the wait. But before long the expert division was up, and I got involved watching the really good surfers do their stuff. Spanky had turned up at the last minute, so the competition was fierce. Wanda, wearing a wild purple wetsuit, looked great in the women's division.

Boy, did those surfers have some radical moves. They carved up the waves, making turns that looked impossible. And Thrash was obviously better than anyone. My respect for him grew as I watched him. He was calm and in control, and he looked completely happy out there in the surf.

At the end of the day, a huge group of very tired surfers gathered around the judges' table to hear the results. Dad, Carol, Jeff, and Sunny had joined me, and I think they were even more nervous than I was about who would win in the women's beginners division.

The judges announced the men's beginners first. Then it was time for my division. "First prize," said one of the judges, "goes to Katie Bear." Sunny glanced at me with sympathy, but I shrugged. No way had I expected to win *any* prize, much less first. But guess what? I won *third*! And let me tell you, walking up there to accept that yellow ribbon was one of the proudest moments of my life.

There was no doubt in my mind — or anyone's probably — that Thrash would win the overall prize for best surfer. And sure enough, he did. He didn't get a ribbon, though. Instead, he got a big fat check. He held it up and waved it over his head. "See you all Down Under!" he shouted, grinning. He gave me a special wink, and I winked back.

What a day. I was exhausted — and starving. That night, Dad took us out to dinner at my favorite vegetarian restaurant. I ate all of my dinner and some of Sunny's, too. Later, as we were driving home, I returned Jeff's lucky penny. "Thanks a lot," I said. "It definitely worked!"

CHAPTER 15

Monday

Dear Mom,
    I miss you! I wish you
could be here with me.
Sorry I haven't written
much lately, but I've been
really busy. I helped to
solve this incredible mystery—
but I'll tell you more about
that next time we talk.
And guess what? I won
a prize in the surfing contest!
I'm enclosing the ribbon I
won. I'd like you to have it
for awhile. At least until
I'm back in Stoneybrook,
that is!
                    Love you
                        —Dawn

I figured it was safe to write my mom, now that the mystery had been solved and the contest was over. If I had sent her the kinds of bulletins I'd been sending to my friends over the past few weeks, she would have been worrying her head off. I would probably never tell her *all* the details of the mystery, but now I could share some of it with her.

Life was pretty much back to normal. I was studying hard for a math test at school. Sunny and I were still busy with the beach program. She was surfing again, carefully, and I surfed with her. I was kind of relieved that the competition was over, so we could just surf for fun and not worry about practicing.

I hadn't seen Thrash since the contest, and I figured he had already left for Australia. And of course, nobody had seen the surfer ghost since the contest. As I said, life was back to normal.

On Friday evening, the kids at the beach program put on their play. Stephie and I sat in the audience and applauded wildly for the actors. The parents loved the play, and the kids seemed to have a great time acting it out, especially Erick, who made a terrific Mad Hatter. Alyssa and Sondra had done a great job with the script and the costumes, and Sunny's sets were perfect.

The following day, I was finishing up at the beach program when I spotted a familiar figure walking along the beach with a surfboard. Thrash. He was still around, after all. I waved to him, and he waved back. Then, to my surprise, he ran to me. "Hey, Kelea," he said. "Congratulations! You did really well in the competition."

"So did you," I said. "You were awesome."

"Thanks. And, hey — thanks for your help. I was definitely on the wrong track, messing with that guy's board. You set me straight. I wouldn't let too many people talk to me the way you did, but I'm glad you were there."

I smiled. "Wasn't it better to win fair and square?"

He laughed. "Definitely."

"So, I thought you were headed for Australia," I said.

"I am. I'm leaving tomorrow. In a few days, I'll be hitting the surf Down Under. Maybe you'll get there, too, someday. You'd like it, Kelea." He smiled at me. "You know, I'm kind of a loner. I've never been used to having friends. But I think you were my friend, and I think I learned something from that. I wanted to thank you." He paused. Then he did something that really surprised me. He pulled the snake ring off his finger and handed it to me.

"I want you to have this, to remember me by." He tossed it to me.

"Wow!" I said. The ring felt heavy in my hand. I tried it on, but it was much too big for any of my fingers. "I'll put it on a chain and wear it around my neck," I said. "Thanks, Thrash. I won't forget you."

"Cool," he said. "Well — later!" He turned and trotted off. I watched him go, knowing I would never again meet anyone quite like him.

That night at home, I found a chain to put the ring on. Standing in front of the mirror, I hung the chain around my neck. The ring looked special and mysterious, and I knew I would treasure it.

On Monday I came straight home from school and headed for the phone. I dialed Claudia's number, knowing it was a meeting day, and my friends would be gathered in her room.

"Baby-sitters Club!" said Kristy, answering the phone.

"Hello," I said, trying to sound ultra grown-up. "This is Mrs. Heidendorferman. I'd like to arrange for a sitter for my triplets, Larry, Moe, and Curly."

"Hi, Dawn," said Kristy, cracking up. It's hard to fool her, but it's easy to make her laugh.

"How *are* you guys?" I said. "You can't believe how much I miss you!"

"We're fine, and we miss you, too. The meeting's just breaking up, so you can talk to everybody, if you want."

"I want, I want," I said. Dad had agreed to let me make this phone call after I had promised to do some extra chores. I was determined to get my money's worth.

"Congratulations on solving that mystery," said Kristy. "And *double* congratulations on winning the contest. We knew you could do it!"

I heard clapping in the background, and my friends' voices calling, "Yea, Dawn!"

"So," said Kristy. "How's the We Love Kids Club? Is business good?"

"Very good," I said. I told her about a picnic we were planning.

In the background, I heard Claudia say, "Kristy, come on! Let *us* talk to her."

"Did you hear that?" Kristy asked. "I guess I better pass the phone around. See you!"

Stacey grabbed the phone next. "Hi, Dawn!" she said. "So tell me, was this guy Thrash cute or what?"

"He was cute, I guess. But he wasn't really my type. Too old, for one thing." Stacey is so boy-crazy sometimes. "But there are a lot of cute guys on the beach," I added. "And they

142

all ask about you. They say, 'Hey, where's that friend of yours from Connecticut?' "

"They do *not*," said Stacey, giggling. "How would anybody remember me?"

"Just kidding," I said. "Too bad you couldn't be in the contest, Stace. I bet you would have won something."

"I don't know about that," she said. "But we sure are proud that *you* did. Anyway, I better go. Claud's about to tear the phone out of my hand!" I heard a shriek, and then Claudia was on the line.

I talked to her for a couple of minutes, and then the phone was passed to Shannon, and then to Jessi. It was so great to hear their voices. I asked Jessi how Mal was doing, and she said she thought it wouldn't be too long before she was back to normal.

Finally, Mary Anne got on the phone. "Hi, sis!" she said. "How's the California ghostbuster?"

"I'm great! How are you? How's Tigger? How's Logan?"

"Everybody's fine. Your mom hung the ribbon you won over the fireplace. She's so proud of you."

"What else is going on?" I asked. I was hungry for news from Stoneybrook.

"Not much. Just the same old stuff, I guess."

I heard somebody shout in the background,

"Tell her about the Arnold twins!"

Mary Anne laughed. "Did you hear that?" she asked. "I can't believe nobody told you yet."

"What happened?" I asked. "Are they still sticking together like glue?"

"Not exactly," said Mary Anne. "Get this: They had a big fight, and now they aren't speaking to each other!"

I cracked up. "After all that," I said. "What was the fight about?"

"Neither of them even remembers. But they each swear the other one started it."

"Of course," I said. Just then, Dad came into the room, pointed at his watch, and raised his eyebrows. "Um, Mary Anne," I said. "I guess I have to go. Dad's giving me the signal."

"Okay," she said. It was great to talk to you. I miss you, sis!"

"I miss you, too. You and everyone in the BSC. But I'll be back in a few months."

"I can't wait."

"Neither can I," I said, feeling a little sad all of a sudden. It was hard to be so far away from my friends and my stepsister. " 'Bye!"

After I hung up, I puttered around my room for awhile, thinking. I smiled to myself when I remembered what Mary Anne had told me about Marilyn and Carolyn. I knew they wouldn't stay angry at each other for long. They were too close. After all, they're best friends as well as twins.

I glanced down at the ring Thrash had given me. It hung on the chain around my neck, reminding me of him. I hoped Thrash would have a best friend one day, so he could find out how great friendship can be.

Friendship. There's nothing like it. Getting to know a loner like Thrash had made me even more grateful for the friends I have, both in Stoneybrook and in California. They are friends I will *always* have, no matter where I live. That makes me one lucky person!

About the Author

ANN M. MARTIN did *a lot* of baby-sitting when she was growing up in Princeton, New Jersey. She is a former editor of books for children, and was graduated from Smith College.

Ms. Martin lives in New York City with her cats, Mouse and Rosie. She likes ice cream and *I Love Lucy*; and she hates to cook.

Ann Martin's Apple Paperbacks include *Yours Turly, Shirley*; *Ten Kids, No Pets*; *With You and Without You*; *Bummer Summer*; and all the other books in the Baby-sitters Club series.

Look for Mystery #13

MARY ANNE AND THE LIBRARY MYSTERY

"Awesome!" shouted Nicky, watching the first fire fighters jump off the truck and run into the building. The kids seemed to forget their fear as they took in every detail of what the fire fighters were wearing, what they carried, and how they attached their hoses to the fire hydrants on the sidewalk near the entrance of the library.

"This is so cool," said Rosie.

Kristy and I exchanged glances. We didn't think it was cool at all, but it was better not to let the kids focus on how awful a fire in the library could be. We agreed, without speaking (best friends can do that, you know), not to say a word to the kids.

It didn't take the fire fighters long to put out the fire — in fact, they never even had to use the hose they had hooked up. Hand-held fire extinguishers seemed to be enough. And soon Kristy and I and all the kids were back in the children's room. I was helping Rosie find those books she had wanted, while Kristy stayed in the office area, talking with Ms. Feld and Mrs. Kishi, who were discussing the fire.

Kristy and I walked Rosie home that afternoon, and then she and I headed to Claudia's for the BSC meeting. Along the way, she told me what Mrs. Kishi had said. "It was a bigger fire than the other one," she said, "mainly because it was started with lighter fluid. It was in a garbage can right outside the back door of the children's room. You know, the door that hardly anybody uses? The one that leads to the back hallway? It's lucky it didn't spread."

"It sure is," I said. "Is Mrs. Kishi worried?"

Kristy nodded. "That part about the lighter fluid obviously scared her. It seems like somebody's getting serious about these fires."

"I just can't believe it," I said. 'Who on earth would want to burn down a library?"

"I don't know," said Kristy. "But I think we need to find out."

We had a mystery on our hands, and it was time to get to work on solving it — before the town of Stoneybrook lost its library.

Super Specials:

9 *Starring the Baby-sitters Club!*
The Baby-sitters get involved onstage and off in the SMS school production of *Peter Pan*.

#10 *Sea City, Here We Come!*
The Baby-sitters head back to the Jersey shore for some fun in the sun!

Mysteries:

9 *Kristy and the Haunted Mansion*
Kristy and the Krashers are spending the night in a spooky old house!

#10 *Stacey and the Mystery Money*
Who would give Stacey counterfeit money?

#11 *Claudia and the Mystery at the Museum*
Burglaries, forgeries . . . something crooked is going on at the new museum in Stoneybrook!

#12 *Dawn and the Surfer Ghost*
When a local surfer mysteriously disappears, Dawn fears his ghost is haunting the beach.

#13 *Mary Anne and the Library Mystery*
There's a Readathon going on and someone's setting fires in the Stoneybrook Library!

Special Edition (Readers' Request):
Logan Bruno, Boy Baby-sitter
Has Logan decided he's too cool for baby-sitting?

by Ann M. Martin

More titles... ➤

The Baby-sitters Club titles continued...

❏ MG45658-X	#57 Dawn Saves the Planet	$3.50
❏ MG45659-8	#58 Stacey's Choice	$3.50
❏ MG45660-1	#59 Mallory Hates Boys (and Gym)	$3.50
❏ MG45662-8	#60 Mary Anne's Makeover	$3.50
❏ MG45663-6	#61 Jessi's and the Awful Secret	$3.50
❏ MG45664-4	#62 Kristy and the Worst Kid Ever	$3.50
❏ MG45665-2	#63 Claudia's ~~Freind~~ Friend	$3.50
❏ MG45666-0	#64 Dawn's Family Feud	$3.50
❏ MG45667-9	#65 Stacey's Big Crush	$3.50
❏ MG47004-3	#66 Maid Mary Anne	$3.50
❏ MG47005-1	#67 Dawn's Big Move	$3.50
❏ MG47006-X	#68 Jessi and the Bad Baby-Sitter	$3.50
❏ MG47007-8	#69 Get Well Soon, Mallory!	$3.50
❏ MG47008-6	#70 Stacey and the Cheerleaders	$3.50
❏ MG47009-4	#71 Claudia and the Perfect Boy	$3.50
❏ MG47010-8	#72 Dawn and the We Love Kids Club	$3.50
❏ MG45575-3	Logan's Story Special Edition Readers' Request	$3.25
❏ MG44240-6	Baby-sitters on Board! Super Special #1	$3.95
❏ MG44239-2	Baby-sitters' Summer Vacation Super Special #2	$3.95
❏ MG43973-1	Baby-sitters' Winter Vacation Super Special #3	$3.95
❏ MG42493-9	Baby-sitters' Island Adventure Super Special #4	$3.95
❏ MG43575-2	California Girls! Super Special #5	$3.95
❏ MG43576-0	New York, New York! Super Special #6	$3.95
❏ MG44963-X	Snowbound Super Special #7	$3.95
❏ MG44962-X	Baby-sitters at Shadow Lake Super Special #8	$3.95
❏ MG45661-X	Starring the Baby-sitters Club Super Special #9	$3.95
❏ MG45674-1	Sea City, Here We Come! Super Special #10	$3.95

Available wherever you buy books...or use this order form.

Scholastic Inc., P.O. Box 7502, 2931 E. McCarty Street, Jefferson City, MO 65102

Please send me the books I have checked above. I am enclosing $_____
(please add $2.00 to cover shipping and handling). Send check or money order - no
cash or C.O.D.s please.

Name _____ Birthdate_____

Address _____

City_____ State/Zip _____

Please allow four to six weeks for delivery. Offer good in the U.S. only. Sorry, mail orders are not
available to residents of Canada. Prices subject to change.

BSC793

Don't miss out on
The All New

Fan Club

Join now!
Your one-year membership package includes:

- The exclusive Fan Club T-Shirt!
- A Baby-sitters Club poster!
- A Baby-sitters Club note pad and pencil!
- An official membership card!
- The exclusive *Guide to Stoneybrook!*

Plus four additional newsletters per year

so you can be the first to know the hot news about the series — Super Specials, Mysteries, Videos, and more — the baby-sitters, Ann Martin, and lots of baby-sitting fun from the Baby-sitters Club Headquarters!

ALL THIS FOR JUST $6.95 plus $1.00 postage and handling! **You can't get all this great stuff anywhere else except THE BABY-SITTERS FAN CLUB!**

Just fill in the coupon below and mail with payment to: THE BABY-SITTERS FAN CLUB, Scholastic Inc., P.O. Box 7500, 2931 E. McCarty Street, Jefferson City, MO 65102.

- -

THE BABY-SITTERS FAN CLUB

___ YES! Enroll me in The Baby-sitters Fan Club! I've enclosed my check or money order (no cash please) for $7.95

Name _____ Birthdate _____

Street _____

City _____ State/Zip _____

Where did you buy this book?

- ☐ Bookstore
- ☐ Book Fair
- ☐ Drugstore
- ☐ Book Club
- ☐ Supermarket
- ☐ other_____

BSFC593

Create Your Own
Mystery Stories!

MYSTERY GAME!

WHO:	Boyfriend	WHY:	Romance
WHAT:	Phone Call	WHERE:	Dance

Use the special Mystery Case card to pick WHO did it, WHAT was involved, WHY it happened and WHERE it happened. Then dial secret words on your Mystery Wheels to add to the story! Travel around the special Stoneybrook map gameboard to uncover your friends' secret word clues! Finish four baby-sitting jobs and find out all the words to win. Then have everyone join in to tell the story!